Praise for Kate Hoffmann
from *RT Book Reviews*

The Charmer
"Hoffmann's deeply felt, emotional story
is riveting. It's impossible to put down."

Your Bed or Mine?
"Fully developed characters and perfect pacing
make this story feel completely right."

Doing Ireland!
"Sexy and wildly romantic."

The Mighty Quinns: Ian
"A very hot story mixes with great characters
to make every page a delight."

Who Needs Mistletoe?
"Romantic, sexy and heartwarming."

The Mighty Quinns: Teague
"Sexy, heartwarming and romantic...
a story to settle down with and enjoy—
and then re-read."

Dear Reader,

When my editor asked me to write a book for the Wrong Bed series, I wanted to find a new and unique setting. I needed a bed and a way to get my hero and heroine into it, but beyond that I knew I wanted to set it in the north woods of Wisconsin. But where? A resort? A luxurious vacation home? A rustic cabin in the woods? Been there, done that!

A comment from my editor brought back a memory of a summer camp I attended when I was in third grade. Even now, I recall the excitement of getting on the bus and traveling to this wonderful place where we had the whole day set aside for fun. I was all about weaving and leatherwork, but it wasn't hard to see what the older girls liked about camp—boys.

Sometimes ideas for a romance novel can come from the tiniest sliver of a memory. I enjoyed going back to summer camp while writing this book, and I hope it brings back some memories for you, too.

All the best,

Kate Hoffmann

Kate Hoffmann

NOT JUST FRIENDS

TORONTO NEW YORK LONDON
AMSTERDAM PARIS SYDNEY HAMBURG
STOCKHOLM ATHENS TOKYO MILAN MADRID
PRAGUE WARSAW BUDAPEST AUCKLAND

Recycling programs
for this product may
not exist in your area.

ISBN-13: 978-0-373-79685-4

NOT JUST FRIENDS

www.Harlequin.com

Printed in U.S.A.

ABOUT THE AUTHOR

Kate Hoffmann began writing for Harlequin Books in 1993. Since then she's published sixty-five books, primarily in the Harlequin Temptation and Harlequin Blaze lines. When she isn't writing, she enjoys music, theater and musical theater. She is active working with high school students in the performing arts and lives in southeastern Wisconsin with her cat, Chloe.

Books by Kate Hoffmann

HARLEQUIN BLAZE
279—THE MIGHTY QUINNS: MARCUS
285—THE MIGHTY QUINNS: IAN
291—THE MIGHTY QUINNS: DECLAN
340—DOING IRELAND!
356—FOR LUST OR MONEY
379—YOUR BED OR MINE?
406—INCOGNITO
438—WHO NEEDS MISTLETOE?
476—THE MIGHTY QUINNS: BRODY
482—THE MIGHTY QUINNS: TEAGUE
488—THE MIGHTY QUINNS: CALLUM
520—THE CHARMER
532—THE DRIFTER
546—THE SEXY DEVIL
579—IT MUST HAVE BEEN THE MISTLETOE...
    "When She Was Naughty..."
585—INTO THE NIGHT
641—THE MIGHTY QUINNS: RILEY
647—THE MIGHTY QUINNS: DANNY
653—THE MIGHTY QUINNS: KELLAN
675—BLAZING BEDTIME STORIES, VOLUME VI
    "Off the Beaten Path"

HARLEQUIN SINGLE TITLES
REUNITED
THE PROMISE
THE LEGACY

To Brenda, my editor, who is always patient and insightful and the best person I could ever have in my corner. I couldn't do it without you!

1

This is page one in my camp jernal. I am ten years old and this is my first summer at camp. I got this book from Gina, my camp consiler, who is really cool and says we should write down what we think. I think there are lots of kids at camp and I hope I make new friends. My cabin is Woodchuck. I sleep in the top bunk. But what if I don't make any friends?

THE WARM BREEZE filled the car with the scent of pine woods and inland lakes. Julia McKee drew a deep breath through her nose and smiled as a familiar excitement began to grow inside her. Even after all these years, it was still there, that mix of nervousness and elation that came in the last miles to Camp Winnehawkee.

She remembered the exact moment her mother had handed her the camp brochure. It had been the summer after her parents' divorce and Lorraine McKee had been unable to cope with the stress of raising her five children. So she'd decided to spend the summer with friends in California.

Julia's four older brothers had been shipped off to sports camps and Julia was put on a charter bus bound for the northwoods of Wisconsin, the brochure clutched in her sweaty hand. She'd read the cover so many times she could recite it by heart. She'd been just ten years old and terrified of what the summer would hold. Friendships for a lifetime? What did that mean?

She really didn't have many friends at home. Julia spent most of her time hiding out in her room, avoiding the incessant bullying of her rowdy brothers. And at school, she preferred reading to socializing, earning her the nickname "Bookworm."

Julia squinted against the oncoming headlights of a car, then glanced over at the clock on the dashboard of her Subaru wagon. A late start and a traffic jam in Chicago had left her two hours behind schedule. At this rate, she would arrive at Winnehawkee just before midnight.

She reached over and picked up her cell phone from the passenger seat, then dialed the number for Kate Carmichael Gray, her very best friend from all her years at camp. They'd been cabin mates that first year, along with Frannie Dillon. Over the following eleven summers, they'd formed a lifelong friendship that had survived another seven years apart.

Kate had married another counselor, Mason Gray, and they'd both lived in Madison before moving to northern Wisconsin when they bought the camp. Mason was a high school history teacher and Kate, a social worker.

Kate's voicemail picked up and Julia sighed. "Hey, Kate. Hey, Mason. I'm still about an hour away. I know it's late and you guys have probably been working hard all day long s go to bed. I'll see you in the morning. I'll find a bunk in one of the cabins. I think I remember how to rough it. Talk to you soon."

She hung up the phone, then wondered if she ought to try calling Frannie. She was supposed to arrive earlier that day with another old camp friend, Ben Cassidy. They both lived in Minneapolis now and had jumped at the chance to help out Kate and Mason.

"We're for you, Camp Winnehawkee, friends forever more," she sang softly. "Every summer we're together, makes us love you more."

She'd graduated from camper to counselor the summer after her senior year in high school, and throughout college she'd returned to the camp each summer as the arts and crafts teacher and advisor for the Woodchuck cabin of twelve- and thirteen-year-old girls.

The camp had been the closest thing she'd had to a stable family. Her brothers had never wanted anything to do with her and she'd rarely seen her father after the divorce, except when he was required to take her for her birthday weekend. And her mother had lost all interest in raising a daughter once she'd begun to date again.

Over the last few years, she'd often thought about the camp. She'd kept in touch with both Kate and Frannie. They'd called on birthdays and holidays and got together once a year for a girls' weekend. But now they were reuniting to bring the camp back to life.

Winnehawkee had closed six years ago. The previous owners had retired to Florida and left the camp abandoned. Rather than sell to developers, they'd insisted that the new buyers reopen the camp. In fact, they'd even written it into the sales agreement. But there were no takers, until Mason and Kate had decided to use the money they'd saved for a house to make a down payment on a little corner of their childhood.

"Though the miles may come between us, we'll never be afraid. For in our hearts, dear Winnehawkee, the friendships never fade."

The camp was reserved in late July for a youth church retreat, but before Mason and Kate could open the gates, they needed to secure another bank loan or find some investors who'd be willing to pay for some of the major improvements. So they'd called on old camp friends to make the trip north, hoping that friendship, nostalgia and a little bit of curiosity would provide them with a workforce ready to make the camp habitable again.

Her cell phone rang and she picked it up.

"Win—ne—who?" Kate's voice called from the other end of the line.

"Win—ne—hawkee!" Julia replied, remembering the little cheer they did after morning meetings.

"Who are you?" they chanted together. "Winnehawkee Winne-who? Winnehawkee. Are you true? Winnehawkee. We're true blue. Winnehawkee, Winnehawkee, whoo!"

"I'm sorry I missed your call. I was just getting Derek and Steven set up in a cabin."

"Derek and Steven are there?" Julia asked.

"Yes." Kate lowered her voice. "And they're now a couple."

"Derek and Steven?"

"Umm-hmm. They own a construction firm in Green Bay and they brought a lot of tools, a trailer full of building supplies and two cases of very expensive wine."

"Who else is there?" Julia held her breath. She wasn't sure she wanted to hear his name. Adam Sutherland. There, she'd said it—or thought it. Adam Sutherland. The memories came flooding back and she felt like her heart was about to burst into a million pieces. She knew he and Mason were still friends. There was always a chance.

"Just them," Kate said. "There'll be more coming tomorrow. And I think Frannie and Ben might arrive in the morning. I made up Woodchuck for you and Frannie. I knew you'd want to be close to the bathrooms."

"Old Woodchuck," she said. "I wonder if—" Julia cleared her throat, brushing the memory aside. "Well,

I'll see you in the morning then. Go to bed and get a good night's sleep. I hope you have your tennis racquet, because we have to play this week."

"I haven't played in years, and we haven't put up the new nets yet, but I'm ready," Kate said. "By the way, I'm counting on you to do some baking for us. I can't be responsible for feeding eight people all week long."

"I have pies in the back of my car. And pastries and croissants for breakfast tomorrow morning. I even made a little Winnehawkee cake for dinner tomorrow night. It looks just like the lodge."

"That's perfect! We have a wonderful dinner planned for tomorrow night," Kate said. "Not the usual hot dogs and baked beans."

"Good," Julia said. "I'll talk to you in the morning."

"Night, Jules. And thanks so much for helping out with this. Mason and I really appreciate it."

Julia hung up the phone and stared out at the road ahead of her. Eight people. Kate and Mason, Frannie and Ben, Steve and Derek and her. Who was the eighth? Could it be *him?*

She'd met Adam Sutherland her third summer at camp. Even as a twelve-year-old, he'd been every tween's dream. With his dark hair and pale blue eyes and his devastating smile, every girl at camp had fallen in love with him at first sight. But for Julia, it had been just the start of a decade-long romance, entirely unrequited and yet as real as any she'd ever experienced.

She'd seen him once since leaving camp eight years

ago. He'd been strolling down Michigan Avenue right
before Christmas with a beautiful woman on his arm.
She knew he worked in finance at his father's venture
capital company in downtown Chicago. She'd looked
him up on Google a number of times over the years,
piecing together a fairly comprehensive biography. She'd
even found a few photos that had been taken at charity
events around town.

Though the infatuation had faded long ago, the curiosity was still there. And when her dating life seemed to
be at its lowest point, she'd wonder what it might have
been like if she'd been able to attract the attention of a
guy like Adam.

As a teenager, she'd put all her thoughts about him
in her camp journal which she'd hidden beneath a loose
floorboard in Woodchuck cabin. She remembered the
day she began the journal at age ten and then the day she
left camp for the last time, the journal still in its hiding
place. She'd walked away from Winnehawkee determined to forget the journal *and* Adam Sutherland. She
thought by leaving the record of her adolescent angst
behind, she'd finally have the closure she so desperately
needed.

But even now, after all these years, she thought of
Adam whenever she thought of Winnehawkee. Julia giggled softly. Gosh, she'd been a fool for that boy. She'd
tried so hard to avoid him, pretending that he meant
nothing to her. And whenever she did attempt to attract

his attention, she managed to make a complete idiot of herself.

There was the time she stuffed the top of her swimsuit with toilet paper, only to get pushed in the water and watch her newfound bust line float away. And then there was the time she made him a lopsided birthday cake in the camp kitchen—she'd tripped on a tree root carrying it to his cabin, splattering the purple frosting over the front of her T-shirt.

But the worst experience, the one that ranked number one in the pantheon of embarrassing moments was when she'd finally poured out all her feelings in a letter. She'd screwed up her courage and left it beneath the pillow of his bunk. Then she learned that he'd switched bunks with a cabin-mate just that week. Dougie O'Neill spent the rest of the summer following her around, trying to kiss her, certain that the letter had been meant for him.

As counselors, she and Adam had worked together regularly, but she'd always kept her distance, treating him like a friend. Hiding her feelings for him, especially when he'd managed to charm nearly every other female counselor, had been one of the hardest things she'd ever done in her life, but it kept her from further humiliation.

Julia moaned softly. Thankfully, her luck with men had gotten a bit better over time, but the results had stayed the same. She enjoyed the fantasy of love, the possibilities and the anticipation, much more than she every enjoyed a real relationship. Men just never lived up to her expectations, at least not the men she met.

Julia suspected her insecurities and disappointments were probably rooted in her parents' divorce, but she told herself that she just hadn't met the man of her dreams yet. When he came along, she'd know and then everything would make sense. Love would finally become a reality.

Over the next thirty miles, her thoughts remained mired in memories of her years at camp. So much of it was good, and even in the worst of times, there had always been dreams of Adam Sutherland to keep her going. Would the journal still be there? Perhaps if she read it again, it might give her more insight into why her love life was so messed up now.

After graduating with a degree in art, she'd fallen into a job as a cake decorator at one of Chicago's most popular patisseries. A few years ago, she'd struck out on her own, building a successful boutique bakery and wedding cake business. But in two months, she was going to begin the adventure of her life, moving to Paris to study pastry making with one of her mentors.

Jean-Paul had been a teacher first, a friend second, and after she'd finished pastry school, a lover. Though they'd shared a passion for baking, that passion had never really taken off in the bedroom.

In truth, her expectations between the sheets had always been more than the men in her life were able to deliver. Where was the frantic need, the overwhelming attraction, the sense that sex was a release instead of merely an enjoyable activity? She'd always wanted to be swept away by lust and then love. But it had never happened.

Maybe she'd meet a handsome Frenchman in Paris and have a torrid affair. She certainly hadn't met many eligible men working in the wedding industry. She was so ready to just throw caution to the wind and indulge, to forget about all of her past mistakes. For once, she wouldn't think about love. She'd think about pleasure first. After all, when in Paris…

But before all that could happen, she needed to say good-bye to the old Julia McKee, the girl who pined after the boy of her dreams for ten long summers. Then, she'd pack her things, leave Chicago and say hello to a new and improved Julia McKee.

Julia focused on the road, following the familiar route to the camp, surprised that she was able to remember it after so many years. But as she got farther from the small towns, the landmarks were less familiar. She watched the GPS on the dash and slowed as the car approached the road that led to the camp.

And then it was there, the familiar yellow and brown sign. It had recently been painted and reflected the headlights from the Subaru. Julia found herself smiling, remembering how happy she'd always been on that first day.

When she reached the main lodge, she noticed that the lights on the wide porch were still on, but the windows were dark. She looked up the hill toward Wood-

chuck cabin and noticed that Kate had kept a light burning for her there, too.

The cabin slept eleven, ten campers in bunks and the counselor in a comfortable double bed in a separate alcove. It was the only luxury that being a counselor provided. Living 24/7 with ten teenage girls was exhausting. A soft bed and a bit of privacy was an absolute necessity.

Julia grabbed her bags from the back of the car and climbed the rise to the cabin. The woods were so peaceful, the wind rustling in the trees overhead, the sounds of crickets filling the air with a kind of summer concert. She could smell the lake on the breeze.

Julia hadn't realized how much she'd missed this place. It was easy to get caught up in the chaos of big city living, accepting the stress and the confusion that came with it. But here, all of that fell away and her life became simple again, like it had been when she was younger.

The inside of the cabin was exactly as she'd remembered it, lit by a globe on the ceiling fan. There were brand-new mattresses on the bunks and the counselor's bed and the place smelled like it had just been scrubbed clean. Kate had thrown open the plank shutters to allow the breeze to pass through and a june bug buzzed against the screen.

It was nearly midnight and Julia was exhausted from the drive. She quickly stripped out of her clothes and pulled on a faded camp T-shirt, leaving her legs bare.

If Frannie arrived later, she'd have to settle for one of the bunks. They could flip for the bed tomorrow.

Julia walked over to the first set of bunks, then bent down to peer beneath it. Was her journal still there after all these years? Or had someone found it? Julia sat back on her heels, suddenly bone tired. She'd leave it for tomorrow. After all, it was just a silly account about a boy she didn't even know anymore.

She pulled the chain on the light. A soft golden glow from the yellow porch bulb still filtered inside, just enough to avoid a stubbed toe. Julia crawled between the cheap cotton sheets and pulled the faded comforter up around her chin with a sigh of contentment. Then she remembered her camp encounters with bats. At least once a summer, a nighttime intruder had driven them from their cabin. She grabbed her tennis racquet and set it on the bed beside her.

As she closed her eyes, Julia let the stress from the ride north fade into sleep. But an image of Adam Sutherland drifted through her head. With a low groan, she rolled over and punched the pillow. She was twenty-nine years old, yet there were times when she still felt like a kid.

BY THE TIME Adam pulled into the narrow driveway for Camp Winnehawkee, it was almost 3:00 a.m. He'd thought about stopping along the way and grabbing a motel room, but he'd been anxious to put the miles behind him and see the camp again.

Yellow lights lined the wide porch of the main lodge

and he could see some of the camper cabins deep in the woods. Though most alumni might not appreciate the quiet of the camp at 3:00 a.m., Adam had spent a lot of early morning hours sneaking in and out and avoiding the demerits that came with breaking curfew. By the time he'd made counselor, he knew all the tricks and handed out a large share of the demerits himself.

A lot of Adam's big life events had happened here at Winnehawkee—his first kiss, his first cigarette, his first sexual experience. He'd lost his virginity on a blanket in the middle of the woods to an older girl from a nearby town. Winnehawkee boasted a wholesome experience, but Adam knew better. He'd used the summers to escape from his parents' stifling expectations and experience a few of life's pleasures.

Like many of the kids at camp, he came from a privileged background—his father was the CEO of a venture capital firm and his mother, a North Shore socialite. He'd attended an exclusive prep school in a wealthy Chicago suburb and had been groomed from birth to take over the family business.

After college, Adam had wanted to go his own way, but family pressure had forced him into working for his father. Though it could have brought them closer together, it had only driven them further apart. As he'd grown more and more frustrated with the company's blind pursuit of profit, his relationship with his father had deteriorated.

Mason and Kate had it right. They wanted to turn

Winnehawkee into a place that would help disadvantaged children, not provide summer babysitting services for rich kids from the Chicago suburbs. There was a time when Adam had imagined he might do work that really mattered, but that dream had dissolved under the burden of family obligations and expectations.

But he'd begun to formulate a plan, a plan to simplify his own life. After he helped Mason get the camp on solid financial ground, he'd find a new future for himself, something that didn't revolve around money and the acquisition of expensive toys. He wasn't sure what that future would be yet, but he was ready for a big change.

He had enough money in his investment account to live a comfortable life for a number of years. Hell, he could just dump the entire portfolio and donate it to Mason and Kate, and still find a way to make a living. Life just wasn't about profit and loss…return on investment…acceptable risk. There had to be more to it.

Winnehawkee had been a refuge for him. A place where he could become his own man. Now it was time to pay that forward. What had happened to that idealistic guy he'd once been? He'd bowed to family obligation and then grown used to all the benefits of a big paycheck. He was on the way to becoming his father.

Adam pulled up next to a Subaru wagon with Illinois plates and wondered who else would be spending the week. Though the cabins weren't the most luxurious accommodations, Adam was looking forward to reliving his younger days. There were beautiful hiking trails to explore around the lake as well as canoeing and swimming. And big campfires at night.

Not knowing what to expect, he'd brought along a sleeping bag and tent, but then noticed a light over the door of one of the cabins. Mason had mentioned inviting a few other guys to help out. Sharing a cabin with them would be much easier than setting up his tent in the dark. He grabbed his overnight bag and headed up the hill. If he could catch a few hours of sleep, he'd be ready to start work first thing in the morning.

The screen door creaked as he pulled it open and he squinted to see inside with only the wash of light from the bulb over the door as illumination. He set his bag down, then sat on the edge of one of the bunks. He hadn't realized how small they were until now.

Adam glanced over to the small alcove that held the bed for the counselor. Though the bedding looked rumpled, he could lay his sleeping bag down and at least stretch out. He walked over and sat down on the edge of the bed. Shrugging out of his jacket, he tossed it behind him. A moment later, he heard a scream. Something hit him on the side of his head and Adam jumped up and spun around.

"Bat. Oh, God, bat." In the dim light he made out the figure of a woman, flailing a tennis racquet around her head. She made contact again, this time with his forehead.

"Ouch!" he cried. "Stop that. There's no bat."

She went still for a moment, then screamed again, tumbling off the far side of the bed and landing with a thump on the floor. Adam searched the cabin for a light switch then finally found the string hanging from the ceiling fan. He pulled it and walked back to the alcove.

She was still there, sitting on the floor, the tennis racquet pulled up against her chest and her hair covering half her face. As their eyes met, he heard her gasp softly. "I'm not a bat," he said, rubbing his head.

"I—I can see that," she replied in a feeble attempt to appear unfazed. She slowly got to her feet, tugging at the hem of her T-shirt to cover her bare thighs. When she brushed the hair from her face, he felt a hint of recognition.

The lush mouth was the same as he remembered. And those beautiful dark-lashed eyes that always seemed to be regarding him with disdain. But the mousy brown ponytail was gone, replaced by shoulder-length waves and a caramel blond color. "Jules?" He laughed. "It's me, Adam Sutherland."

"Adam," she said, a nervous smile twitching at her lips. "Right. I—I didn't know you'd be coming."

"Mason didn't mention you'd be here either," he said. His gaze took in her features. In the past eight years, she'd changed, and all for the better. He'd always liked Julia McKee, but the feeling had never been mutual. Adam had found her smart and funny and guileless. Too bad she'd never given him the time of day.

In truth, he suspected that Julia disapproved of his

reputation with the ladies. She was the one girl in camp that he'd never been able to charm—and here she was, all grown up, incredibly sexy and sleeping in his bed.

"So, how have you been, Jules?"

She blinked, as if startled by his inquiry. Hell, it wasn't his best attempt at an opening line. But what else was he supposed to say to the girl he used to fantasize about? Adam stretched across the bed and held out his hand to help her up.

Ignoring his hand, she scrambled to her feet, then sat down on the edge of the mattress and pulled the sheet up around her, her gaze still fixed on him. "I'm fine," she said.

He nodded. Well, this was awkward. He felt compelled to smooth things over before he excused himself to find another place to sleep. "I just assumed that they'd left the light on for me. I didn't realize you were in the bed or I wouldn't have…"

Her expression finally relaxed and she smiled again, this time with much more warmth. "I'm sorry I hit you. I felt something on my face and I thought it was a bat. I remember them being very partial to this cabin in the past."

"You have quite a forehand."

"Actually, it was a backhand. Did I hurt you?" She reached out to touch his temple and the moment she made contact, Adam felt a current race through him. He swallowed hard, then reached up to take her hand, twisting his fingers through hers. "I—I'm sure I'll recover. I'm sorry I woke you. What time did you get here?"

She stared down at their fingers, still tangled together. "Just after midnight." She yanked her hand away. "What time is it?"

"Three in the morning." He frowned. Why had that felt so good? He hadn't expected such a strong reaction to such an innocent touch. "I was exhausted—until you hit me. Now, I'm wide awake." Wide awake and looking for any excuse to keep her talking. "And hungry. Are you hungry?"

She tipped her head to the side, regarding him with a mix of confusion and amusement. "I guess I could eat," she said.

"Breakfast would be good. Are there any all-night diners around here? I could run out and get us something."

"You're not in Chicago. I don't think we'd find an Ashland Grill up here."

"You know the Ashland Grill? I love that place," Adam said, grinning.

"It's not far from my flat."

"You live in Chicago?"

She nodded. "Yeah. I do."

"I guess I remember Mason mentioning that," Adam said. "Where?"

"Wicker Park."

"Lincoln Park," he said. "Right near the river." He couldn't believe they'd been living so close and he hadn't even known. It made sense. Her family was from the Chicago area. But it was odd that their worlds probably intersected at least a few times a week and yet he'd never thought of her. Why hadn't he thought of her? What had Julia McKee been doing with her life?

"I have something," Julia said. She jumped out of bed and ran to the door, her bare feet soft against the rough floor. "I'll be right back."

"Where are you going?"

"To my car," she said.

The screen door slammed and Adam walked over to it, watching her scamper down the hill. Her T-shirt flew up as she ran and he caught sight of bikini panties and the sweet curve of her backside. He imagined the body beneath the shirt, soft and naked, made for his touch.

She stubbed her toe on a tree root and stumbled, cursing loudly in the quiet night. He stepped out of the door, ready to go to her aid, but she continued on, limping the rest of the way.

Adam chuckled to himself. It had been a long time since he'd been so intrigued by a woman. Imagine running into Julia after all these years. Though she'd grown even more beautiful, she was still the nervous, clumsy girl he remembered. And yet, in a single instant, all the old curiosity came back. Julia McKee was a challenge, the kind that he usually found irresistible.

This was going to be a very interesting week.

JULIA'S EYES WATERED as she limped to the car. "Please don't let him be watching," she murmured over and over. She was afraid to look back, worried he'd be standing there on the front steps of the cabin, observing her clumsy stumble down the path.

When she reached the car, she realized she'd forgotten her keys. To her relief, she'd left the back door open after removing her bags. Julia crawled over the backseat and reached for the bakery box. If he was hungry, then she'd feed him. "Cinnamon buns," she murmured, drawing in the scent.

She found the canvas bag that had her coffee supplies in it—her French press, the gourmet coffee they served in the bakery and an electric pot to heat water. She grabbed a few bottles of water and her car mug, then headed back to the cabin, this time careful to avoid the bumps in the trail.

"Don't mess this up," she murmured. "Just be cool."

"Do you need some help?"

She glanced up to find him standing in the middle of the path. God, he was so incredibly sexy. And charming. And funny. And all those crazy feelings that she'd had as a teenager were back again—only much worse…or maybe better. "Take the box," she said.

"What is all this?"

"Breakfast. You said you wanted something to eat."

"You carry breakfast around in the back of your car? Just in case you…" He shook his head. "I can't think of any reason why you'd do that."

"I'm a pastry chef and Kate asked me to make some things for breakfast. And I have to have my coffee in the morning, so I always travel with my own stuff for that."

He held the door open for her, then followed her inside. She set her coffee supplies on one of the bunks, then found the single electric plug beneath the mirror on the wall. Julia glanced over at him to find him watching her. "You can open the box. Help yourself." She filled the pot with bottled water and then plugged it in.

He opened the white container and looked inside. The scent of yeast and cinnamon wafted through the air. "Are these cinnamon rolls? Oh, my God." He pulled one from the box and took a bite, smearing cream cheese frosting on his upper lip. She caught herself staring, wondering what it would be like to lick it off very, very slowly.

"You made these?" he asked, his mouth full.

"It's what I do," she said, trying to keep from leaping for joy. There were times when food—really good food—could be considered a form of foreplay. Right now, she wanted to imagine him experiencing the ultimate pleasure from eating her cinnamon buns. If she was lucky, the other pleasures would come later.

Adam sat down in the center of the big bed, crossing his legs in front of him. "Are you sure we should be eating these? Will Kate be mad?"

"There are croissants and apple tartes in the car. I brought plenty."

"You should go into business," he said. "These are really good."

"I have my own business. I own a pastry shop."

"I guess I'm in real trouble then," he said, staring at her in disbelief. "You're beautiful and you can cook."

"Bake," she corrected, feeling a blush warm her cheeks. "I'm really not much of a cook."

She shouldn't let herself fall for his charm. Julia knew it was all part of the package with Adam. With him, every woman was a conquest, every seduction a battle to be won. She crossed the room and sat down on the edge of the bed. "The coffee will be ready in a few minutes."

He watched her shrewdly as he licked frosting off his fingers. "You've never liked me much, have you, Jules?"

His blunt statement took her off guard. Well, at least she'd managed to hide her feelings well. "No. I—I mean, I don't *not* like you." She drew a ragged breath. "Why would you say that?"

"I just always had the sense that you didn't think much of me. We just never…you know…connected."

Julia fixed her gaze on her fingers, clutched in her lap. "I guess I didn't really like standing in line," she murmured.

"Ouch." He laughed softly. "I suppose I deserved that one. You were right, though. A girl like you shouldn't have to compete."

"A girl like me?"

"A good girl," he said. "I—I don't mean good in a bad way. I mean…good. Worthwhile. Hey, I always thought you were pretty cool. I always wished we had gotten to know each other a little better. As friends."

"I guess we'll have time for that this week," she said.

"Yeah, I know I'm going to be sticking pretty close to the woman who makes these cinnamon buns."

Julia giggled, another blush warming her cheeks. He was smooth with the compliments, all right. Still, why not enjoy the attention. What harm could it possibly do now? If she wanted to spend her week flirting with Adam, then she would. And if it went a bit further than that, well, that was fine, too. Why not finally act on her crush? It could be a fantasy come true.

A shiver skittered down her spine. Just the thought of allowing him to seduce her, of falling into his arms and into his bed, made her heart beat faster and her breath come in shallow gasps. She pressed her hand to her chest, feeling her heart pound beneath her fingertips.

"Are you all right?" he asked.

"Coffee," she said, jumping to her feet. She busied herself with the coffee press, filling the bottom with ground beans, then pouring the hot water on top. She found her favorite mug in the box and set it on the floor.

"It feels good to be back here," Adam said, glancing around the cabin. "On the drive up, I felt like I was a kid again. I recognized all the landmarks. And then there's the smell in the air."

"It smells green," she said. "I love that smell."

She poured a cup of coffee for each of them, then crossed the room to the bed. Adam moved down to rest his back against the footboard of the old wooden bed and Julia took the opposite end, tucking her feet beneath her.

The atmosphere felt so intimate, just the two of them, together, the night silent around them. She'd dreamed about a moment like this, wondered what it would be like to have him all to herself. And here he was, the answer to all her teenage fantasies—and most of her adult ones as well.

They stretched out on the big bed, facing each other, the conversation easy between them. Every now and then, his thigh would bump against hers and Julia would feel her heart flutter. She fought the urge to throw aside caution, crawl on top of him and kiss him.

Adam wasn't the kind of guy who'd refuse such an advance. She had no doubt about that. In fact, she could picture in her mind, every moment of every second— the strength of his long, lean body, the warmth of his mouth, the feel of his hands on her. Julia sighed softly, her breath coming out in a tiny moan.

"I'm sorry," he said. "I'm keeping you up."

"No! No, it's fine. Now that I've had my morning coffee, I'm up. There's no going back."

"Funny. I was exhausted when I got here and now I feel like I could run a marathon."

"It's the coffee," she said.

He sent her a crooked smile. "Maybe. Or maybe it's the company?"

Julia gave him a playful kick. He grabbed her bare

foot and held it between his hands gently massaging it. The contact sent a flood of warmth racing through her veins, setting every nerve on fire.

"Yeah, I know. Those cheesy lines don't work on you," he teased. "But you can't blame a guy for trying, can you?"

"No," she said. "I guess I can't."

Their gazes locked for a long moment and Julia's heart skipped a beat. There was an attraction there, in the way he looked her, in the way he smiled. And she wasn't imagining it. Had it always been there? Could she have been so wrapped up in her own infatuation that she'd never noticed?

She smiled and glanced down at her coffee. After that one attempt—the letter that had gone horribly astray—she'd never tried again. But what if she had?

There were many things to regret about her ten-year crush on Adam Sutherland. But she was through with regrets. From now on, she was going to take chances and damn the consequences. And if she made a complete fool of herself, she'd just run off to France and hide for the next two years.

2

Year three at Camp W. I've decided that I will put all my secrets in this book. And the one secret I want to write first is that HE IS THE CUTEST BOY EVER. Way cuter than Luke Perry. Tomorrow, I'm going to talk to him. And before the summer is over, he is going to kiss me. My life will never be the same again.

ADAM OPENED HIS eyes to the morning light filtering through the trees. Raking his hand through his hair, he sat up and looked around the cabin. Julia was gone, her side of the bed neatly made. He smiled to himself as he stretched his arms over his head and yawned.

He couldn't remember the last time he'd spent a night in bed with a beautiful woman and nothing had happened between them. But then, maybe leaping into a physical relationship upon first meeting wasn't such a bad idea. Where had that gotten him in the past? Sure, there'd been a lot of great sex, but nothing much beyond that.

He was almost thirty. The big three-oh. And he wanted more from life than just a series of shallow relationships with beautiful, but brainless, women. He wanted a challenge, a woman who wouldn't melt in his arms and tell him everything he wanted to hear. He wanted someone who'd keep him interested for more than a few months.

Hell, Jules had kept him interested for ten years. And now that she'd reappeared in his life again, Adam realized that the interest hadn't waned. He swung his legs off the edge of the bed, working the kinks out of his neck as he retrieved his duffel bag.

He'd probably missed breakfast, but if he was lucky, he'd find a cup of coffee and some of Julia's leftover pastries to get him through until lunch. But he really wasn't interested in food. He wanted to see her again.

He found a pair of faded cargo shorts in his bag along with an old T-shirt, then stripped out of his jeans and polo shirt. As he dug through the contents for a fresh pair of boxers, he heard the screen door squeak.

Adam slowly turned to find Julia standing in the doorway, a mug of coffee in her hand. Just the sight of her was enough to make him grin like a goofy school kid. She was dressed in a pale blue camisole, a flowing cotton skirt and a pair of sandals that revealed perfect toes painted in a bubblegum pink.

Though she was a pastry chef, it didn't look like she

ate much of her work. She was slender and long-limbed, with a body that he longed to touch. "Morning," he said. "Is that for me?"

"It is. Everyone has been wondering about you. I told them you got in early this morning, after I was up." Her gaze slowly drifted down his body as she approached, the mug wrapped in her outstretched hands.

Adam smiled. He liked that she stared. She was interested enough to look. Curious, maybe? They'd have a whole week together and he didn't want to waste another moment. Adam wanted to know more about her, to spend some time together, to see where this attraction might lead. Yet he knew he ought to be patient. Jules wasn't the kind of woman who jumped into bed without careful consideration of the consequences.

"I guess I fell asleep," he said, taking the coffee from her. "I probably should have taken one of the bunks but—"

"It's all right," she said, shifting nervously from foot to foot. "Nothing happened. You were the perfect gentleman."

"Lucky you couldn't read my thoughts," he said taking a step toward her. She didn't move away and Adam took that as a good sign. He brought his hand to rest on her waist and smoothed his palm over her hip. Then, he slowly bent closer and brushed his lips against hers.

The kiss was a test, he reasoned. If she reacted negatively, then he knew exactly where he stood, but if she...

An instant later, Julia threw her arms around his neck and returned the kiss. But this wasn't a test. This was a full-on, tongue-tangling passionate kiss.

Adam stumbled slightly, the coffee sloshing onto his hand and scalding him. With a groan, he dropped the mug and it smashed on the wooden floor. But the kiss easily distracted him from the pain in his hand. He grabbed her waist and pulled her along to the bed and they fell onto it, her body coming down on top of his.

He cupped her face in his hands, trying to slow the frantic assault and she softened beneath his touch, then drew back to look down into his gaze. Her eyes were wide and questioning. "Are you all right?" he murmured.

Julia nodded, breathless.

"That was nice. Do you want to try it again?"

She frowned. "Was there something wrong with the first time?"

"Oh, no. There was nothing wrong. Here, let me prove it." Their second kiss was much more relaxed and they lingered over each other's mouths, teasing playfully, tasting deeply. "Who needs coffee when I have you to wake me up?"

She ran her hands over his bare chest, pressing her lips to shoulder in a deliberate trail. "You can't stay here," Julia said. "You have to find another place to sleep."

"I know." She kissed him again and he groaned softly as his hands trailed over her back. He bunched the fabric of her skirt in his fists, pulling it up until her legs were bare. "But that doesn't mean I don't want to stay." He ran his thumb over her lower lip, still damp from his kiss. "What if I come back in the middle of the night when no one is awake? I'm really good at sneaking through camp without getting caught."

She nodded. "You need to come to breakfast. They're going to wonder where I am."

"Only if you kiss me. Once more."

She smiled then leaned down, running her tongue along the crease of his mouth before indulging in one last, long, perfect kiss. Then Julia pushed off of him and stood beside the bed, clutching her hands in her loose skirt.

"I think we should keep this between the two of us," she said. "I don't want to be the talk of Camp Winnehawkee."

Adam nodded slowly. He was going to let her set the terms for now. "All right. That sounds reasonable."

She walked to the screen door, then paused before she turned back around. "I've always wondered what that would be like," she said. "Kissing you. Back then, you kissed a lot of girls at Camp Winnehawkee."

"The only one I really wanted to kiss was you."

"And was I what you expected?"

Adam nodded. "You do know how to kiss, Jules, I'll give you that." He looked down at the erection pressing against the fabric of his boxers, then covered it with his hands. "Sorry. That tends to happen when I get excited."

With a soft giggle, she shoved the screen door open. "Put that away before you come to breakfast."

He moved to the door to watch her as she strolled down the hill. She tripped on the same tree root she had the night before, pitching forward before she righted herself. Hopping on one foot, Julia rubbed her toe and turned back to see if he was watching. "Are you all right?" he called.

"Fine," she replied, giving him a wave.

"Breakfast," he murmured as he moved back to the bed. He grabbed the clothes he'd chosen and tugged them on, then slipped his feet into a pair of boat shoes. Though he was anxious to see Mason and Ben again, there was only one person on his mind right now and she had a sweet mouth and a soft body and a smile that made him crave her more than her cinnamon rolls.

A FEW MINUTES later, once he was sure he was decent, Adam jogged down to the dining hall. When he walked inside, he found all his old friends gathered around a table near the kitchen doors.

"Well, there he is!" Mason cried. "We were about to send out a search party. We're burning daylight and you're getting your beauty sleep."

Adam crossed the room, grinning at Mason. "I can see you've had a bad case of insomnia. There's nothing pretty about you, Mase." He held out his hand and Mason grabbed it, pulling Adam into a hug.

"Good to see you."

Adam gave Frannie and Ben a wave, then shook

Derek and Steven's hands. "I always thought you two belonged together. I'm happy for you both." He glanced around. "Where can I get something to eat?"

"Kate has everything set up in the kitchen. Grab yourself a plate. Coffee is out here."

As Adam walked to the swinging door, Kate burst through with a tin of maple syrup in her hand. "I found it! I don't know if this is—Adam!" She threw her arms around his neck and gave him a fierce hug. "There are pancakes and sausage in the kitchen. I can make you eggs if you like. When did you get here? Where did you sleep?"

"Late. I brought along my sleeping bag," he replied. He wasn't sure that Jules had explained last night's sleeping arrangements, so he decided to play it cool. "Pancakes will be terrific."

Adam pushed the door open and stepped inside, following Julia back into the huge camp kitchen. Julia pulled a baking sheet out of the old commercial oven. "If you're making more of those cinnamon rolls, I could eat four or five."

She turned around and smiled at him. "Scones," she said. "Raspberry." Julia plucked one off of the baking sheet and tossed it at him. "Be careful, they're hot."

He pulled up a stool and sat down at the huge prep table, dropping the hot scone in front of him. "So what's the plan for today? Can I just stay here and watch you bake, or do I have to do some work?"

"You need to move your stuff out of my cabin," she said.

"Why? Nothing happened last night. I'm sure we can cohabitate peacefully."

"This week isn't about us. It's about Mason and Kate."

"But we're not going to be working all day and night. We'll have time to ourselves. So, maybe we could go into town tonight for dinner? Just you and me?"

She stared at him for a long moment, as if trying to figure his motives. Hadn't he been clear? Or did she simply not trust him? Was he moving too fast, expecting more than she was ready to give. But that kiss. It was all there in that kiss—the need, the longing, the desire. Was he supposed to ignore that?

"You're right," Adam said, picking up the warm scone and biting off a corner. "We need to focus on the job at hand." He held up the biscuit and nodded. "It's good."

With that, he turned and walked out of the kitchen, leaving Julia to think about how she wanted to play this. If he was right about the kiss, then she'd come around to his way of thinking sooner or later. And for a woman like Julia, Adam was willing to wait.

"So, what's on the agenda for today?" he asked his friends, reaching for the carafe of coffee.

"We're re-roofing three of the cabins," Mason said. "The girls are going to be replacing the screens in two of them and then I'm hoping someone will volunteer to wallpaper the nurse's office. The last time Kate and I wallpapered, we almost came to blows."

"I'm good at wallpapering," Julia said as she came out of the kitchen, a basket of scones in her hand.

"Me, too," Adam added. "I'm an expert."

"Good," Mason said. "You two can work on that project tomorrow." He stood and grabbed his coffee mug. "Well, men, it's time to get down to business."

Adam circled the table to Julia and reached for another scone, resting his hand on the small of her back. "Just one more," he murmured.

She glanced at him, her gaze fixed on his mouth, and he knew instantly what she was thinking. Could he steal one more kiss without anyone noticing? "You know, I think I'll wrap up a few of those scones to go."

"I'll get you a bag," she said. Julia turned back to the kitchen and a few seconds later, Adam followed her through the door.

She spun around when she realized he was in the room with her, her hands braced against the edge of the work table. Adam slowly crossed to stand in front of her. She was so close, he could feel the heat from her body and hear her breath coming in quick gasps.

He slipped his hands around her waist and pulled her against him. Adam didn't bother to ask. He could see what she wanted the moment their gazes met. His mouth came down on hers, and this time, there was no hesitation, no doubt about what it all meant.

They wanted each other and denying it was an exercise in futility. His tongued delved into the warm depths of her mouth and she responded eagerly, matching his desire in every way. Adam's hand skimmed over her hips and he cupped her backside, drawing her even closer.

But there was a limit to what he could take from her before the evidence of his desire was on display for all to see. He stepped back, knowing if he went on, he'd need a cold shower or at least ten minutes alone to recover.

"I'll see you later," he said, letting his palm smooth across her back.

A smile touched the corners of her mouth. "Don't you want your scones?"

Adam shook his head. "No. It will give me a chance to come back.

"Later," she repeated.

When he reached the door, he glanced back to find her still standing where he'd left her, her hand pressed to her chest, her lips still damp from their kiss.

Adam strode through the dining room and out onto the porch. "It's going to be a good day," he said to Mason as they strolled out into the sunshine.

JULIA'S KNEES WOBBLED and she drew in a deep breath, trying to steady herself. But the rush of oxygen only made her dizzy. She stumbled to the sink and splashed some cold water on her face. Would she ever get accustomed to kissing him? Would the after-effects wear off more quickly the more they did it?

Since their kiss in the cabin, she hadn't been able to think of anything else. She'd accidentally dropped two eggs, spilled a glass of orange juice and burned a batch of scones just reliving that moment. And now there was another moment to add to it.

She drew another breath. Though she'd dreamed about kissing him for years, she'd never expected it to have such a profound effect on her. The taste of his mouth, the warmth of his lips, the strength of his hands on her body, were enough singly to drive her to distraction. But combined, she was powerless to do anything but surrender.

When she was teenager, all her fantasies were colored with romance. But now, everything was about raw lust. His touch made her body ache from something more satisfying and she knew exactly what it was. Naked bodies, limbs entwined, searching mouths and soft sighs.

This was exactly what she'd dreamed about and now that it was happening, she wanted to remember every single moment. Slowly, she sank to the floor and closed her eyes. The taste of him was still on her lips and she smiled. Blindfolded, she could kiss a hundred strangers and recognize him.

She wanted to run and jump and scream, letting loose the wild emotions that coursed through her body. But Julia knew that for now, she had to keep her feelings to herself. This could last a day or two and then, just as suddenly as it began, it could be over. And the last thing she wanted to do was make a fool of herself.

And yet, it was so hard to believe it was real when she was the only one who knew about it. If she could tell Kate or Frannie, then maybe it wouldn't seem so surreal. And maybe it wouldn't frighten her so much.

There hadn't been a man in her life that had made her feel this heady mix of elation and anticipation since— well, never. What would happen when she saw him next, when he touched her again?

"Jules?"

She looked up to find Kate standing beside her, the coffee carafe in her hands.

"What are you doing?" Kate asked.

"Nothing," Julia said, scrambling to her feet. "Just… relaxing. I didn't sleep very well last night."

Kate sat down next to her. "Are you all right? You look a little flushed." She pressed her palm to Julia's forehead. "Are you getting sick?"

"No. It's just the heat in the kitchen. The oven's been on. I'm great, really."

Kate sighed. "Sometimes I wonder if we'll ever finish what needs to get done. With everything we cross off the top of the list, we add another two or three on the bottom."

"So, we have to fix the screens on the cabins?"

"Don't worry, it's not that hard. It just takes time and patience. But we don't have to get to work yet."

"What are you guys doing in here?" Frannie said,

wandering into the kitchen. She plopped down on the other side of Kate and leaned over to look at Julia. "Are you all right? Your face is all red."

Julia clapped her hands to her cheeks. "Yes."

"She's just warm," Kate explained. She sighed softly. "I can't tell you how much we appreciate all your help. We just never could have done this alone. And hiring help is beyond our budget. Do you have any idea what plumbers cost these days?"

"It's no problem," Frannie said.

"I just want you to know that—"

"Stop," Julia said, wrapping her arms around Kate's shoulders. "We're all here because we love this place and we love you."

Kate pulled them both into a group hug. "I'm so glad we're all back here, together."

"We haven't changed at all, have we, girls?" Frannie said, stretching her legs out in front of her. "But you know who's gotten better with age?" She leaned over the table. "Adam. Oh, my God, I didn't think he could get any hotter, but he has. Why hasn't some woman snapped him up by now?"

"Maybe he's gay," Kate said. "Look at Derek and Steven. We never even suspected they were."

"I don't think he's gay," Julia said.

"How do you know?" Kate's eyes went wide. "You two haven't—"

"I saw him in Chicago once. On Michigan Avenue, walking down the sidewalk with this gorgeous blond woman. He was definitely into her. It was obvious. I think he just likes women too much to settle on one."

"When a guy looks like that, I guess he can afford to play the field," Kate said. "I still say the best thing to ever happen to Mason was his hairline receding. Marriage looks pretty good to a guy who thinks he's going bald."

Frannie scrambled to her feet. "We need to have a toast."

"It's too early to start drinking," Julia said, getting to her feet. She reached out and pulled Kate up. "We should really wait until at least 1:00 a.m."

"I was going to say noon," Kate countered.

"We're on vacation. We can start whenever we want," Frannie said. She filled three glasses with orange juice and passed them out. "To Camp Winnehawkee. Friends forever."

"It really is true," Julia said. "Look at us. All these years have passed and we're still friends. I don't think I have any better friends than you two."

"We really should get together more than once a year," Frannie said. "After all, we don't live that far apart."

"Well, that's about to change," Julia said. She set her glass down on the prep table and took a deep breath. "I'm moving to Paris with Jean-Paul at the end of the summer."

Her friends stared at her, mouths agape, as if she'd

just sprouted horns and a tail. "With Jean-Paul? As in, you two are going together? As a couple?"

Julia shrugged. "I suppose there's that possibility, but no. We're going for professional reasons. He wants to compete in the M.O.F., so he's going back to work there for a few years in his family's patisserie. He asked if I wanted to come."

Kate frowned. "What's the M.O.F.?"

"The Meilleurs Ouvriers de France. When you're certified M.O.F. that means you're the best. He's the only teacher at the Pastry School that doesn't have the certification and that's because he came to the U.S. when he was just out of school."

"Are you going to live together?" Frannie asked.

"No. We're not even going to work together at first. He's set me up with a very famous pastry chef and I'm going to work in his shop."

"For how long?" Frannie asked.

"I don't know. It could be six months, a year. Two, if things go well. Or I could come back after a few weeks if they don't." Julia shrugged. "I just feel like I need a change in my life."

Kate shook her head. "I don't know, Jules. You had a romantic relationship with this guy a few years ago. As I remember, he wasn't very nice to you. And now you're going to Paris with him. It sounds like it's a bit more than just a professional trip."

"Do you want it to be more?" Frannie asked. "Are you still in love with him?"

"Still?" In love? Julia wasn't sure she knew what it meant. After spending less than a day in the general vicinity of Adam Sutherland, she'd decided that if she could take any man to bed in the entire world, he would be the one. Jean-Paul wouldn't even come in a distant second. "No, I don't love him," she said. "This is just a really great opportunity and I can't pass it up."

"What about the bakery?" Kate asked.

"The bakery will be fine. I have a wonderful manager and plenty of people who will keep it going until I get back." She forced a smile. "I need a change. I need to shake things up a bit. Besides, you guys can come and visit. Think of all the fun we could have in Paris. It's not that far. We could even meet in London or Rome."

"I don't think I'm going to have a lot of extra cash for traveling," Kate said. "We're putting every spare penny into the camp."

"Oh, don't you worry. I have frequent flyer miles that would take us both to the moon and back," Frannie said. "We'll go next spring. Springtime in Paris. It will be perfect."

"Perfect," Julia said. And yet, the thought of Paris didn't seem quite so perfect anymore. Paris was an ocean away from Adam, from this scary, exciting, confusing affair that they'd jumped into. And though it might be over tomorrow, Julia wanted to believe that there might be a chance it would survive their week at Camp Winnehawkee.

She'd never in her life thought it would happen at all.

And now that it had, she didn't want it to end. She drew a ragged breath. So, maybe she'd have two months of unbelievable reality before she'd have to return to her fantasies. Two months to get her fill of Adam. And then she'd go to Paris and make another dream come true.

Still, if all she had was two months, she was going to make sure every day counted.

"OUCH! SONUVA BUNNY."

Adam straightened and set the nail gun down. He worked the kinks out of his neck and back, stretching his arms above his head and groaning softly. He'd been on the roof of Porcupine for over an hour, finishing up the work that he and Mason had begun before Mason had to leave to help Kate with dinner preparations.

Julia was somewhere inside the cabin, working on replacing the screens. And from what he'd been hearing in between the sounds of the air compressor and the nail gun, it wasn't going particularly well.

He walked across the shallowly pitched roof to the ladder and climbed down. Adam found her hunched over one of the windowsills, a hammer in her hand. He watched through the screen door as she tried to pound a small nail into a strip of wood that held the screen in place.

"Sonuva bunny," she cried again as she hit her thumb with the hammer.

"Sonuva bunny?" he said.

Julia jumped at the sound of his voice, then slowly turned to face him. "I guess I'm falling back into old habits. We weren't allowed to swear at Camp Winnehawkee."

"Why would you need to swear?"

"It's the only thing I can do. My carpentry skills are almost non-existent. My fingers are all smashed."

"Can I show you a little trick?" he asked, opening the door.

"If it involves finding a way to make my fingers stop throbbing, I'm listening."

"Well," he said. "First things first." Adam grabbed her left hand and brought it up to his lips, then gently kissed the tip of each finger. "Better?" he asked.

She released a tightly held breath, then shook her head. "Not quite."

He pressed his lips to the center of her palm. "How about now?"

"That feels a little better. But the pain is kind of creeping up my arm."

Laughing, he pulled her into his arms. "And has the pain reached your lips yet?"

Julia playfully pressed her hands against his naked chest. "Almost. Do you have a remedy for that?"

Adam nuzzled her neck, biting softly on the silken skin just beneath her ear. "Don't start something we can't finish, Jules."

"It's just a kiss," she said.

"Maybe this morning it was just a kiss," he murmured. "But I've been up on that roof all morning thinking about you. And I don't want to stop at just a kiss. I don't think you do, either."

"Are you saying that I can't resist you?" Julia asked. "Because I can, if I want to."

He growled softly, dragging his thumb over her lower lips. "No, you can't."

She tipped her chin up at a stubborn angle and re-garded him coolly. "I resisted you for ten years."

"Yes, but that was then. This is now." He leaned for-ward and brushed a kiss across her mouth, his tongue tracing the crease between her lips. Adam had never really put much effort into kissing. It always came quite naturally. But this kiss would put away the last of her resistance.

At the first flicker of submission, he smoothed his hands over her face, molding her mouth to his and deep-ening his assault. He could feel her surrender in the way her body sank against his, her hands clutching at his shoulders.

He shifted his touch, moving his hands over her body in a lazy caress. She moaned as he cupped her breast and her body went soft when he pulled her hips against his, his hard shaft evident beneath the fabric of his shorts. And when Adam felt that he'd made his point, he suddenly stepped back, leaving Julia off-balance.

She stumbled and reached for a nearby bunk, her face flushed and her lips swollen. Wide-eyed, she looked over at him. Drawing a ragged breath, she shrugged.

"All right. Well, I can see you're determined. I'll give you that."

Adam grinned. But when he heard Mason's voice outside, his smile quickly faded. Julia frantically ran her fingers through her tousled hair. He crossed to the window and picked up the hammer, turning his back to the door to hide his erection.

"Adam? Are you in here?" Mason opened the door and stepped inside the cabin.

"He's here," Julia said in a bright tone. "He's just helping me with the screen. I keep hitting my thumb with the hammer."

Adam glanced over his shoulder and nodded. "I'll just be a minute. I'm going to show Julia how to do this so she doesn't keep bashing her fingers."

Mason looked back and forth between the two of them. Adam groaned inwardly. Mason wasn't blind. He knew when someone was trying to hide something. Hell, he was a schoolteacher. Schoolteachers had a built-in bullshit detector.

Adam picked up the needle-nosed pliers and put a small nail between the grips. "See, you can hold the nail with this and then pound. Once it's started, it's no problem." He quickly handed the pliers to Julia.

"Thanks, I'll give that a try," she replied.

"Right," Mason murmured. "Well, carry on, then. Kate says dinner is in a half hour. I'll just be up on the roof until then."

They both watched as Mason walked outside. Neither one of them moved until they heard his footsteps on the roof. "Sonuva bunny," Adam said softly.

"I don't think he suspected anything," Julia whispered. "It wasn't like he caught us doing anything."

"Well, I wish he would have," Adam said. "Sneaking around like this is stupid. We're nearly thirty years old and we're acting like a couple of teenagers."

"This is the way it has to be," she said.

"Why?" Adam asked. "Give me one good reason."

"Because if you decide to dump me after three days, I won't be humiliated in front of all of my friends."

Her words hit him like a slap to the face. Is that really what she thought of him? That he'd be so shallow, so cruel as to seduce her on a whim? Adam stared at her in disbelief, his gaze fixed on hers.

"I'm sorry," Julia murmured. "But I don't want to look like a fool."

"Jules, I would never do that. I care about you." He shook his head. "I—I don't know what to say."

"Don't say anything," she replied. "I'll be fine if this only lasts a week. In fact, that would be perfect. I don't expect more and I'm not sure I want more. But, I don't want my friends assuming the worst about you or me."

"And what is the worst?" he asked.

"That you're a shallow creep and I'm a pathetic loser."

He drew a deep breath, then let it out slowly. Discussing this was going to take a lot more time and privacy than either one of them had right now. But he did intend to address it the very next time they were alone. "I have to go help Mason. We'll talk about this later."

She nodded silently, staring down at the pliers in her hands. Adam reached out and covered her fingers, drawing both her hands up to his lips. He kissed her wrist and she managed to meet his gaze again. "This is not just about sex," he said. "And I would never do anything to hurt you. Do you believe me?"

She paused before she nodded. "You should get going. Mason is going to be wondering what's taking you so long."

With a quiet curse, Adam turned and walked out of the cabin. When he got outside he paced back and forth on the gravel path, fighting the urge to go back inside and set Julia straight. But all the talk wouldn't change her mind. She was working off an image she had of him that was eight years old. He'd have to show her that he'd changed.

He circled the cabin and climbed the ladder, crawling up on the roof, then crossing to where Mason stood.

"Everything all right?" Mason asked.

"Fine," he said. "She just needed a little help."

"Is there something going on with you two?" Mason asked.

Adam shook his head. "No. Why would you think that?"

"Because this roof is pretty thick and the screens are open and you were down there whispering for a long time."

"No, there's nothing going on. That's my official answer and I'm sticking to it."

As he continued to work, his mind returned to the woman fixing screens just below him. Maybe it had been for the best that they'd never started anything all those years ago. Julia McKee was a complex and confounding mass of feminine contradictions. And it was going to take him some time to figure her out.

He had six days and six more nights. If he wanted a chance at success, he was going to have to work fast.

3

I was sure when I finally got boobs he'd notice me. Now that I'm not as flat as a board, he should at least look at me. I'm fourteen. And I've never kissed a boy. Yesterday, when he walked past me in the dining hall, I almost said hello and asked him to sit with me. I took a deep breath and got up, but then my mac and cheese went down the wrong pipe and I started coughing and couldn't stop. Nurse Benson came over and asked if I was all right. I think she was about to give me the Heimler. What good are boobs if no one notices them?

THE BOTTLE OF wine was empty and Julia finished what was left in her glass, then pushed back from the dinner table. She and Kate and Frannie had gathered there after cleaning up the remains of an extravagant gourmet dinner. The boys had stuck around for Julia's dessert—apple custard pie—before taking off on a late-night shopping trip for beer and building supplies.

Julia covered her mouth as she yawned. "I'm going to bed. All this fresh air and hard work has worn me out."

"But we're going to make a bonfire when the guys get back," Kate said. "It's only eight-thirty."

"I didn't sleep very well last night," she said. "And I've got to make some calls. I had orders for a lot of wedding cakes to be delivered today and I want to be certain all the brides are happy." She gave them a wave. "I'll see you both in the morning."

"Night, Jules," they called as she walked out of the kitchen.

The air was still and humid. She drew a deep breath as she stepped out on the porch. It had been a strange day. It had started with a long, delicious kiss and ended with Adam watching her silently from across the dinner table. Since their argument that afternoon, he'd made no attempt to steal a moment, made no mention of when they'd next talk.

Julia had been left to wonder if she'd blown it before it had even begun. It was clear that they shared a powerful attraction. And though it might look like casual interaction to everyone else, she felt it was something much deeper. They'd embarked on an experiment last night that she hoped would continue tonight. But if it didn't, she was prepared to deal with the rejection.

She climbed the hill to Woodchuck cabin and opened the screen door. Adam had moved his things out sometime during the day. It was the proper thing to do. He couldn't continue to live with her—at least not without causing a lot of speculation amongst their friends. But with Frannie choosing to occupy a cabin closer to the water, Julia was assured of at least a little privacy.

She flopped down on the bed and closed her eyes. Visions of a half-naked man drifted through her mind. There was one benefit to the stifling heat. Adam spent most of the day without his shirt. He had grown into the most amazing specimen of male physical beauty that she'd ever seen—wide shoulders, narrow waist, muscles that rippled beneath his tanned skin.

She caught herself staring at him whenever the chance presented itself—when he came in for another glass of ice water, during lunch on the wide porch of the dining hall, when he'd tried to seduce her in the cabin. She'd been careful not to stare for too long. Looking at him was like looking into the sun—dangerous.

But here, alone, she could linger over those thoughts. She could slowly undress him in her mind. Imagine herself drawing down the zipper on his shorts, slowly pushing the faded cotton boxers over his hips, and—

The journal. She'd been so preoccupied all day long that she'd forgotten to look for it. Julia crossed the room and peered beneath the bunk on the far wall, searching for the familiar loose floorboard. It should be exactly where she remembered, yet none of the boards were loose. It was impossible to see anything in the light from the ceiling. She'd just have to look again in the morning.

As she stretched out on the double bed, a june bug bounced against the screen next to her head and Julia jumped. She reached for her tennis racquet, hoping the bug was still on the outside. But then another and another hit the screen until she realized it wasn't bugs but she was hearing but pebbles.

She peered out into the woods to find Adam standing beneath the window. "What are you doing?" she called.

"Getting devoured by mosquitoes," he said.

"Why?"

"I'm trying to get your attention."

"You could knock on the door. That might work."

"I thought you wanted me to be more discreet."

"Just come inside."

He grinned, then disappeared around the corner of the cabin. Julia scrambled off the bed and ran her hands through her hair. Though she'd taken a quick shower before dinner, her skin was sticky from the heat and her clothes clung to her body. But it didn't matter. If things went as planned, she wouldn't have need of her clothes for long.

Adam stepped inside the cabin, the screen door slamming behind him. He crossed the room and pulled the chain on the light, throwing them both into darkness.

Julia's heart pounded in her chest and she found herself holding her breath, waiting for him to approach, to touch her. Perhaps if she took a step in his direction, the impasse would be broken and he'd pull her into his arms and kiss her like he had that morning.

But a kiss or a simple caress wouldn't be enough anymore. She'd spent the day fantasizing about so much more—touching his body, undressing him, falling into bed naked while wrapped in his arms. She swallowed hard, suddenly growing a bit light-headed. "Was there something you wanted?" she asked, her voice wobbling.

He crossed the room in three long steps and pulled her into a kiss, his mouth ravaging hers until she surrendered completely. There was no way she could deny him any longer. The attraction was too overwhelming, the need too acute.

His hands skimmed over her body, the friction delicious through the thin fabric of her clothes. When he cupped her breast in his hand, Julia moaned softly and as he slowly teased her nipple to a hard peak, she felt the need inside her burn. This wouldn't end until they were both naked and he was buried deep inside her.

"I'm sorry about this afternoon," he murmured, his lips warm against hers. "We'll do this any way you want."

Julia slid her hands beneath his T-shirt, her palms skimming over the hard muscle and smooth skin of his belly and chest. Adam drew back, cupping her face in his palms. "Come on, let's go."

She gasped. "Where?"

"I—I want to take a canoe ride. Do you want to come with me?" His request was almost desperate.

She looked up into his eyes, seeing the desire there, knowing how close they'd both come to total surrender. Maybe it was best to find something to occupy their time while the others were still up and moving around. "Sure, that sounds nice."

He took her hand and led her outside, walking carefully down the wide path to the lake. Electric lamps lit the way, but Julia was careful. The last thing she wanted to do was trip and embarrass herself again.

"I love this place at night," Adam said. "It's so peaceful. Like a whole different world." He turned to face her, walking backward in front of her, his feet crunching on the crushed gravel. "I envy Mason and Kate. Changing their lives the way they are. Coming up here to live and work. Do you ever think about just walking away from your old life and starting out new?"

"I do," she said. "I have."

"Me, too." They continued to walk, Adam pointing out dangers in the trail.

They reached the dock and Adam helped her down into one of the old wooden canoes. Then he untied the line and carefully sat down in the stern. He grabbed the paddle and they glided out onto the glassy surface of the lake.

"Is this really what you want to be doing?" she asked.

"No. But I figure the longer we put off the inevitable, the better it will be."

The inevitable. Is that how he saw the two of them? And what would happen after the inevitable took place? Would their curiosity be appeased? Would their hunger be sated? Or would an intimate relationship become like a drug, powerful and addictive.

Julia looked out over the water, fixing her gaze on a light across the lake. She'd decided to move to Paris, to change her life completely, but as they took another step toward full-scale seduction, she realized that this night with him could change her life forever.

THE WATER WAS as smooth as glass and the only sound Adam heard was the soft swish of his paddle as it dipped into the lake. Though the last place he wanted to be was in a canoe in the middle of the lake, it gave him a chance to re-evaluate what he and Jules were about to do.

She seemed to have some doubts about his intentions, though it hadn't really stopped her from plunging ahead. But Adam didn't want this to be another one-night stand. There was something about Julia that made him want more. There was a deeper connection between them than just the physical. And with every intimate caress or lingering kiss, he found himself wanting to slow down and be careful.

Moonlight fell on the lake and reflected up into her pretty features. He studied her profile as she stared out at the water and he knew exactly how the night would end. And yet, he didn't want to rush. When they thought back about their first time together, he wanted the memory to be perfect.

"Why haven't we ever met up in Chicago?" he asked. "I run in to people I know all the time. Why couldn't I have run in to you?"

She tipped her head to the side. "I saw you once. On

Michigan Avenue. It was right before Christmas and it was snowing."

"Why didn't you come up and say hi?" he asked.

"You were with a woman. She was blond and she was wearing a fur coat. Besides, I didn't think you'd remember me."

"I would have remembered," he said. "And I would have been happy to see you."

"I don't believe you," she said, shaking her head. "You don't have to say things like that just to please me, Adam. I don't need to be charmed in order to want you."

"I'm telling you the truth. I used to think you were the coolest girl at camp, Jules. All the other girls were so silly and annoying and you were so…focused. I always wondered what was going on in that head of yours." He paused. "What are you thinking about now?"

"About what happened in the cabin this afternoon," she said. "And what will happen later."

He pulled the paddle back into the canoe then carefully made his way forward, bracing his hands on the gunwales. He sat down in the center seat and grabbed her hands, pulling her a bit closer. "We're all alone here, Jules. Tell me your secrets. Tell me what you need."

"What do you want me to say?"

"That you think about this as much as I do," he replied. "I spent the entire day replaying that kiss we shared this morning. And thinking how I wanted it to happen again. And how I wanted you in my arms and in my bed. Do you want that, Jules? I need to hear you say it."

"Yes," she replied, her fingertips trailing up his arm to his face. She ran her hand through the hair at his nape and he felt his skin prickle with goosebumps. She barely had to touch him and he felt a familiar tightening in his groin. Adam leaned forward and brushed his lips against hers, pulling her between his legs.

The moment they made contact, she leaned forward, shifting her weight. The canoe rocked and Julia, surprised by the sudden movement, tried to straighten and regain her seat. Adam grabbed her hips to pull her back down, but when he did, she lost her balance and landed on the gunwale, throwing the canoe over to one side.

With a tiny scream, Julia reached out for him but there was nothing he could do to prevent her from going over the side, short of falling in with her. In a tangle of limbs, they hit the water.

They both popped up at the same time and Adam turned to find the canoe upside down behind them. He looked back at Julia and helped her brush the strands of wet hair from her face. "Are you all right?" he asked.

"Yes. Apart from being wet, I'm fine."

He chuckled as he helped her wipe the water from her face. "Usually I'm so much better at this."

Julia swam over to the side of the canoe. "What are we going to do? Can you tip the canoe back over?"

If it had been a lighter aluminum model, it might be possible. But the old wooden canoes were heavy and it would take more than the two of them to right it. "Probably not. We're not that far from shore. We can swim for it."

"Swim?"

"The water's warm, we'll just take our time. I used to swim across the lake at least two or three times each summer. It'll be fun."

"What about the canoe?"

"We could drag it back, but that would take a while. I'll just come out early tomorrow morning and haul it back in."

"You're the one who talked me into kissing you in a canoe and look what happened. I haven't been swimming in years. I'm not even sure I can make it to shore."

"It's not my fault we capsized. You're the one who stood up."

"You're saying it's my fault?"

He grabbed her around her waist and pulled her against him, bringing his mouth down on hers. "I'm saying we should make the best of this." He reached down and unzipped his shorts, then pulled them off and held them out in front of him. "You might want to take off your skirt. It'll be a lot easier to swim." Adam pulled off his T-shirt next, then tossed the clothes on the upturned canoe. He kicked away and floated on his back, staring up at the starry sky.

"I really don't know if I can swim that entire way," she said.

"Don't worry. I'll save you if you can't. I'm a certified lifeguard."

"I'm sure you say that to all the girls," she murmured. "Next, you'll offer to give me mouth-to-mouth."

"This is the first time I've ever ended up in the water during a canoe ride," he said.

Julia took off her skirt and tossed it next to his wet clothes, then began to swim toward shore. Adam swam beside her as they headed for the light at the end of the Winnehawkee dock. This wasn't exactly what he had in mind for their first full night together, but she seemed to take the accident in stride.

They reached the raft first, moored about fifty yards from the shore. Adam climbed the ladder, then helped Julia up. She flopped down on the plank surface, throwing her arms out to the side and gasping for breath. He laid down beside her. "We'll just rest here for a bit."

She wiped the water from her face and sighed deeply. Adam rolled onto his side and stared down at her. "Kiss me," he said.

"Are you sure you want me to do that? Bad things seem to happen when I kiss you." She held out her hands. "Will the raft sink?"

"No," he murmured.

Her fingers lazily following the line of hair that ran from his collarbone to his belly, Julia bent forward and pressed a kiss to his chest, then gently moved her mouth to a spot just below his ear. It was all he could do to enjoy the moment. In his mind, he wanted to strip off the rest of their clothes and lose himself inside of her. But a slow, easy seduction would take time—and patience.

He reached out and ran his fingers along her rib cage to her breast. Her breath caught and she seemed to tremble at his touch."Are you cold?" he asked.

"No."

"Maybe you should get out of those wet clothes," he teased. To his surprise, she pulled the camisole up and over her head, leaving her body naked above the bikini panties she wore. It was a blatant invitation that Adam wasn't about to refuse.

He chuckled softly, grabbing her by the waist and pulling their bodies together in a warm embrace. They kissed for a long time, hands touching, mouths tasting, the raft bobbing with each movement. He moved down to her breast, teasing at her nipple with his tongue until it grew to a hard peak.

"You have the most beautiful body," he murmured. "The most perfect breasts."

"You noticed," she murmured.

His hand cupped her flesh and Julia arched against him, her body writhing with every caress. He ran his fingers through her wet hair, then kissed her forehead, his lips warm and damp. He found her mouth and she tasted sweet and warm, her tongue teasing at his, her naked torso pressed against his chest.

He'd enjoyed a lot of unusual experiences at Camp Winnehawkee, but this was a new one for him. He'd never had sex on the swimming raft before. He pushed up and glanced back at shore, wondering if they could be seen, wondering if he really ought to worry. Adam grabbed Julia around the waist and pulled her on top of him, drawing her knees up along his hips and kissing her deeply as their bodies shifted against each other.

She was nearly naked and he hooked his thumb in the waistband of her panties, the thought of her completely vulnerable to his touch too much to resist. She reached down and a moment later kicked the panties off.

"Better?" she asked.

He held his breath as he touched her, reveling in the feel of her naked flesh beneath his hands. He wanted to take everything slowly, to savor each moment. But Julia was impatient. Her hair tumbled around her beautiful face and he watched as she pressed a line of kisses to his naked chest, moving lower and lower until she reached his belly.

Adam knew the power of her touch on his body. He wore only his boxers and they clung to the hard ridge that had sprung up the moment he kissed her. Gently, she stroked him, wrapping her fingers around his erection. Adam closed his eyes and groaned, arching into her touch. When she looked up again, his gaze met hers and he watched her every move.

He wasn't sure what it was—their wet bodies, the sight of her naked in the moonlight, the gentle rocking of the raft—but it all felt so incredibly new and so erotic. "You look like a water nymph sent to tempt me," Adam murmured.

Julia smiled, pulled his boxers down then dipped lower and took him into her mouth. Her touch was a shock to his body and he jerked, sucking in a sharp breath. She continued to caress him with her tongue and her lips, carefully gauging his reaction and drawing him away from the edge again and again. And when he couldn't last much longer, she stroked with her hand until he dissolved into a powerful orgasm.

Wave after wave of pleasure coursed through his body. In the past, sex had always been a wonderful physical release. But this was more. This was an experience shared, a surrender to a desire that couldn't be controlled. He'd never really felt the kind of passion that he knew he ought to feel, until now.

Slowly, his body returned to normal, the spasms subsiding, the intense pleasure dulling and his breath coming more evenly. The sticky result of the intimacy was spattered across his belly and he smiled.

"Look at what you've done," he murmured.

Julia leaned forward and ran her tongue along the crease of his mouth. He reached out and drew her into a long and sensuous kiss, his lips and tongue communicating his pleasure without words. Adam reached between them to touch her and the moment he did, she moaned softly. She was already wet and when he slipped his finger into her heat, she cried out in pleasure.

He wanted to possess her completely, to bury himself

inside her and bring them both to a climax together. But the condoms he'd put in his pocket—his *only* two condoms—were floating somewhere in the middle of the lake right now and he wasn't about to go look for them.

When the first spasm shook her body, he nuzzled her neck, whispering to her, urging her on. And when her shudders had subsided, Adam gathered her in his arms, his fingers tangled in her hair.

He pressed a kiss beneath her ear. "You realize this changes everything. I can't go the whole week pretending this never happened. How am I supposed to be around you now? How can I keep from touching you and kissing you every time you're near?"

"Let's not make it complicated," Julia said. "It doesn't feel real yet."

"And when it does?"

"Then we'll tell everyone. But we don't know what's going to happen or even if this will last until the end of the week."

Though Adam wasn't sure why it was so important to her, he had no choice but to agree. Maybe she was right. If it was just the two of them, there were fewer expectations, fewer questions. And he knew the odds. Though he wanted to believe in true love, it didn't happen often. And it had never come along in his lifetime.

"How am I supposed to swim back to shore?" Julia murmured. "I'm not sure I have functioning limbs anymore."

"I could go get another canoe," he suggested.

"We could sleep here," she teased.

"Or I could swim back and get that inner tube and I'd push you back to shore."

She stood up and stretched her arms above her head. The sight of her naked body in the moonlight was enough to put his senses back on alert. "Wow," he murmured.

"I'll race you back," she said. With that, she dove into the water.

Groaning, Adam sat up. He wasn't sure what the rest of the night would hold, but he was willing to swim another fifty yards to find out.

JULIA LAY ON her side, her naked body covered with the sheet from Adam's bed. They'd swum back from the raft and ran through the woods to the Otter cabin where Adam had taken up residence. The swim had cooled them off and with the fan, it was comfortable in the cabin.

"So, I guess you like me now," he murmured, idly playing with a strand of her hair.

"I guess I do." That was the understatement of the century. But though Julia had decided to throw all caution to the wind when it came to Adam, there was still a part of her that maintained a healthy suspicion.

Adam Sutherland enjoyed the pursuit. If a girl was too easy to catch, he lost interest. For her own sake, it would be best to play it cool—or as close to cool as she could.

"And when we get back to Chicago at the end of the

week, maybe I could take you out to dinner? On a real date?"

"We'll see. Maybe we should just...see."

He rolled over on his stomach and stared down into her eyes. "You're not just using me for sex, are you?"

Julia saw that, though his tone was teasing, the question was one that required an honest answer. "No. I like you."

"I like you, too, Jules."

She sighed softly, then curled into his body. "I'm glad we got that settled."

"You know, you never gave me the time of day when we were younger. I used to think you hated me."

"I didn't trust you," she said. "Besides, I didn't want to be another notch on your bedpost. You were quite the camp Casanova. How many girls were there?"

"Fewer than you'd think. And you're not afraid to be a notch on my bedpost now?" he asked.

"Maybe you're a notch on *my* bedpost," she said with a smile.

"So you *are* just using me for sex. I knew it."

Julia pushed him back into the pillows, then crawled on top of him. "Maybe just a little. But I do think you're charming and funny. And I am a little curious about what happened to the guy who used to run through pretty girls like clean socks."

He gave her a strange look. "I don't know what happened to him. Sometimes I wonder myself. Here with you, this is the first time in a long time that I've been completely…content."

She sighed softly, then laid back down next to him, throwing her leg over his hips. "This is kind of nice."

"Did your life turn out the way you wanted it to, Jules? Have all your dreams come true?"

Julia nodded. "For the most part. I'm happy. I have a job I love. I don't have a lot of time for a social life, but that's my fault. I suppose I could make more time if I really wanted to." She ran her finger along his lower lip.

"Me, I have a job I hate. And you know why I hate it? Because all I'm doing is making a lot of money for guys who already have a lot of money. When Mason and Kate decided to buy the camp, Mason came to me and asked me to help him get financing for the camp and I promised him I'd find it for him. He wants to do something really useful here and yet, no one I know will even consider giving him the money he needs."

Julia frowned. "Does he know this?"

"I haven't said anything yet. I'm hoping after we get the place fixed up, maybe a local lender might come forward, but there are some powerful people in this area that want him to fail."

"Why?"

"Because he's sitting on lakefront property, Jules. Acres of beautiful undeveloped property. And it's the perfect place for a builder to put up million-dollar vacation homes or a new resort."

"But Kate told me that couldn't happen. It's in the sales contract."

"Well, Mason and Kate can't subdivide. But if they go bankrupt and the bank forecloses, then the new owners might be able to do whatever they want. There are legal ways around it." He smoothed the hair back from her face. "I have a lawyer from my firm looking at all the documents. We're thinking about setting up a foundation and keeping the land in trust. It's all really complicated. He's going to call me later this week."

"What else can we do?"

"There's nothing you can do," he said. "It's the economy. Places like this barely make enough to survive. It's just not a very profitable enterprise. Luckily, they both have regular jobs. Mason will teach and I'm sure Kate can find a position as a social worker."

"Are you always so pessimistic?" Julia asked.

"I'm just being realistic, Jules. Making this a camp for really rich kids brought in a lot of money. If you're going to serve underprivileged kids, then you have to find some way to generate revenue. If the money won't be coming from the parents, where will it come from?" He sighed. "Do you know anyone with an extra $100,000 sitting around?"

She thought about it for a long moment. "I probably do. Some of my clients are very wealthy socialites in Chicago. They do charity work and I've donated a lot of my time to their causes. Maybe I could call in a few favors."

He sat up, bracing his hand behind him. "If you could do that, I can draft a proposal. If you can get them to come up here and see the place, meet Mason and Kate, then maybe we can make this happen for them." He leaned forward and kissed her. "Could you call them? Tomorrow morning?"

They spent the next hour talking about Adam's plan. And with every minute that passed, Julia felt as if she was getting to know the man that Adam had become. He was much more complicated than she'd first believed and not nearly as egotistical as she assumed. His concern for Mason and Kate, his desire to make their dreams come true, was noble and kind, and Julia found her reserve wavering.

Would it be so bad to fall in love with him all over again? She could do a lot worse. And it's not like there was a future for them. But they could have these next few months together. And for her, that would be enough.

"I think we can do this, Jules. We're going to have to work fast, but I think we can make this happen." He smiled. "We make a pretty good team, you and me."

"Except in a canoe."

"Well, considering you are a bit clumsy, I probably shouldn't have taken you out without strapping you to the seat."

"I'm not clumsy," she said. "And you're the one who tried to seduce me in the canoe. Whose fault is that?"

"Come on, Jules. You have to admit you're a klutz. What about that time you were carrying that cake and you tripped and fell on top of it. It's all right that you're clumsy. I find it very...endearing."

Julia felt her cheeks warm with embarrassment. He knew about the cake? But he hadn't been there. Did everyone know it was for him? She crawled off of him and began to search for something to wear. "I—I don't remember any cake," she murmured. "What time is it? I should probably get back to my cabin."

"No," Adam said, reaching out to grab her hand. "Stay here for the night. You can sneak out in the morning. I promise, I'll wake you up and walk you back to Woodchuck before anyone else is up."

She stared down at him. How did she ever get here, she wondered. Standing naked next to Adam's bed, contemplating whether she ought to spend the night or go back to her own bed. Never in her life had she been so impulsive, so reckless. She thought this would be all about satisfying her curiosity. If she seduced Adam, she could finally close that chapter in her life. But now that she'd gotten to know him again, she wasn't satisfied with a chapter. She wanted to read the rest of the book. Maybe she even wanted a happy ending. And she definitely wanted to have sex—real sex—with him.

"I'm sorry I called you clumsy," Adam said. "In fact, I think you're the most beautiful, graceful, seductive woman I've ever laid eyes upon."

Julia laughed. "Now you're just lying."

"I'm not," he said with a wicked grin.

"Yes, you are. You think if you say things like that I'll come back to bed."

"We haven't finished what we started," he suggested.

"And who says we have to do everything in one night?"

She bent down and picked up one of his T-shirts from the floor and pulled it over her naked body. He groaned softly, flopping back on the bed and throwing his arm over his eyes. "Note to self. Don't call new girlfriend clumsy."

Julia's breath caught in her throat. Is that how he thought of her—as his new girlfriend? She turned to walk to the door, stunned by his statement and unsure of what to make of it. It was nothing, just a casual comment, she thought. "I'll see you in the morning," she said.

"You're a cruel woman, Jules," he shouted.

As she walked back to Woodchuck, Julia couldn't help but smile. It had been the night of her dreams, a fantasy turned into reality. And yet, it had been so much more. There was a real connection between them. But was it just the excitement of being back at camp, of indulging in something that would have been impossible years ago? Maybe he was as curious as she had been.

Goosebumps prickled her skin and she felt a thrill race through her. There was no going back now. They'd stepped off the edge of the cliff and indulged their fantasies. What would tomorrow bring? Julia pressed her palm to her chest. She could barely wait to see.

4

Boys can be so dumb sometimes. I can't figure out how their brains work—if they even have brains. My mother says that intelligence always beats beauty. But how is a guy ever going to know you're smart if they never talk to you. I think if you want to catch their attention, you have to be pretty first. I'm wearing my new dress to the dance tonight. And I'm thinking about dying my hair blond. My mother would kill me, but I don't care. There has to be some way to get him to notice me.

THEY SAT AROUND an old wooden table that Kate had dragged out to the wide porch of the dining hall. Lunch had been a simple meal of barbecue sandwiches, potato salad and coleslaw, washed down with cold beer and iced tea. Adam leaned back in his chair and took a long sip of his beer, watching Julia as she stirred a spoonful of sugar into her tea.

He chuckled softly. She was so careful not to show

any interest in him when they were around the others. But he wasn't quite so adept at ignoring his attraction to her. Whenever he had the chance, he sat down next to her or brushed up against her or shared a whispered greeting.

In truth, all the sneaking around added another layer of excitement to the whole affair. But he didn't harbor any illusions that they'd be able to continue like this for long. He wanted to spend his nights with Julia, in her cabin, in her bed, and he didn't care who else knew about it. At some point, the cat would have to get out of the bag, but for now, he could wait.

"Did Mason show you what we found in Possum?" Ben asked.

"Oh, wait," Mason said. He reached into his pocket and pulled out a Matchbox car. "Look at that. A hot pink Beatnik Bandit. Do you know how much things like this go for these days?"

Kate reached over the table and took the car, examining it closely. "Where did you find it?"

"Stuck up in one of the rafters. When we pulled the plywood off the roof, there it was."

"How much do you think it's worth?" Julia asked.

"Well, it's one of the Sweet Sixteen collection and in a very rare color, so I—"

"How does he know so much about toy cars?" Frannie asked.

Kate rolled her eyes. "He still has the Hot Wheels collection his dad gave him."

"It's our nest egg," he said. "I could sell it and send our children to college. Well, maybe not to college, but I could buy them a decent used car."

"How much is this one worth?" Julia asked.

"A hot pink Beatnik Bandit sold for seven thousand not too long ago. This one isn't mint and with the economy the way it is, the collectible market has crashed. I'm not sure. I'll have to look it up."

"If only we could sell all the other junk we've found." Kate got up and walked into the office, then returned with a cardboard box. "Godzilla finger puppet," she said, holding it up. "Whoopee cushion. Scooby-Doo Pez dispenser—broken. A good one fetches three hundred on eBay, my husband tells me. Oh, and this." She pulled out a bound book with a flowered cover. "We found this under a floorboard in Woodchuck. It's not worth anything, but it is the most pathetic account of unrequited love ever to be recorded at Camp Winnehawkee. I'm thinking we might be able to get it published."

"Can I see that?" Julia asked, standing up to grab the book from the center of the table.

But Adam grabbed it first and flipped it open. "Who wrote it?"

"There's no mention of a name," Kate said. "I read through the whole thing. The boy she refers to only as A." Kate grinned. "I suppose that could be you, Adam. As I remember, you did get around back then. Oh, and she got the book from a counselor named Gina. Do any of you remember her?"

"Can I see it?" Julia insisted.

"I'll know if it's about me," Adam said. "Here. Let's read a bit of it, shall we?"

Julia pushed away from the table. "You know, I'm going to drive into town and pick up the wallpaper for the nurse's office. Does anyone want to come with me?"

"Oh, here's a good part," Mason said, grabbing the book from Adam. "When I see him, my heart begins to beat faster. I wonder if he ever thinks about me, if he ever notices me. Yesterday, I ran into him when he was coming out of the dining hall and my water bottle fell on his bare foot. He picked it up and smiled at me. His hand even touched mine when he gave it back to me. I thought I would die." Mason groaned dramatically. "I thought I would die," he cried, slamming the book shut.

"Stop," Frannie said. "The poor girl probably spent her whole summer pining after some boy she could never have. That's kind of sad."

"Or pathetic," Ben said.

"More than one summer," Mason said, flipping through the pages. "The book goes on for five or six summers at least. Maybe more."

"We should try to figure out who it belongs to and get it back to her," Kate said. "If it was mine, I'd want it back."

Adam glanced over at Julia. Her gaze darted nervously between Mason and Kate. "I really have to go. The wallpaper is at the hardware store in town, right?" Julia asked, an impatient edge to her voice.

"No," Kate said, "it's at the building supply store on the way out of town."

"I'll drive you," Adam offered.

"I'm sure I can find it myself," Julia said.

Adam stood up and circled the table, then jogged down the front steps. When she didn't follow, he turned back to look at her. "Come on, let's go."

Reluctantly, Julia followed him to his car. He opened the passenger-side door of the BMW for her, then circled around to the driver's side. A few moments later, he was steering the car down the narrow drive to the main road.

What luck, this rare opportunity to have some time alone with Jules without having to sneak around in the dark. And he might even have a chance to finally pick up some condoms. "So, where should we go? We've got at least an hour, maybe two."

Julia stared out the front window, barely listening to him. He watched her for a long moment, but he couldn't read her mood. She wasn't angry. But she wasn't exactly happy either. "Are you all right?"

"What?" She glanced over at Adam.

"What's wrong?"

"Nothing. I was just thinking."

"About me, I hope."

She rolled her eyes. "I don't spend my entire day thinking about you," she said.

"Is it that book Mason was reading?" he asked.

"No, why would that upset me? I feel badly for the person who wrote it."

"Why?"

"You've never had to live through unrequited love. You've always managed to have whomever you wanted. You just crook your finger and the girls come running. It isn't always that easy for the rest of us."

"How did this become about me?" he asked.

"It isn't."

Frustrated, Adam pulled the car to the side of the road and threw it into Park. Then he leaned over the console and took her face between his hands. He kissed her softly and then with more intensity and he felt her resistance melting beneath his touch. When she finally wrapped her arms around his neck, he knew that whatever had been bothering her was now in the past.

"So, should we just find a private place to park or should we rent a motel room for a few hours." But before they did anything, he'd have to find a drug store of a motel gift shop to supply his share of condoms. With Jules, he was going to need it.

"I've never done it in a car," Julia murmured, glancing around.

"I know the perfect place."

She giggled. "I'm sure you do."

He put the car in gear again. "It's not far. Just down the road. We can hit it on the way back." But when he reached the old logging road, Adam noticed the row of mailboxes. What was once a deserted spot in the woods had been developed over the past eight years. "I guess not," he murmured. "I guess we'll need to look for a motel."

When they got out to the highway, Adam headed toward town, but every motel they passed had a No Vacancy sign lit. The finally saw a vacancy sign when they passed the Whispering Pines, an old-fashioned motel with small cottages instead of a row of rooms.

But Julia shook her head. "No, this one doesn't look right. It's too...old."

He sat leaned back into the leather seats. "Why don't we go get an ice cream cone," he murmured.

"That sounds like a good idea," she said.

He groaned inwardly. What had happened between last night and now? Sex was all she could think about last night, but now, she was happy to settle for ice cream. He glanced over at her, wondering what had happened to preoccupy her.

His thoughts returned to the book. Could he be A.? Was that why she was upset? He trolled his memory, searching for a hint of the incident mentioned. But though it might have been important to the writer of the journal, he didn't remember anything of the sort happening to him.

Though he wasn't ashamed of his reputation back then, he could understand how it might bother Julia. The last thing she needed was a reminder that he had been known as the camp Casanova. "Ice cream it is," he said.

Her mood seemed to lighten considerably as they drove into town. The warm breeze flowed through the open windows of Adam's car. It was a perfect summer day and given their situation, he would have preferred to have her all to himself, on a quiet beach or bobbing on a boat in the middle of the lake.

There were moments when he felt as if nothing could come between them but then, at other times he sensed how tenuous their bond actually was. They were together now because of Mason and Kate. What would happen when they returned to Chicago? Would that all change?

The ice cream stand in the small town of Boulder Lake was a throwback to the fifties. It was more of a shack than a shop, with wide wooden shutters that opened to a view of the small operation inside.

They used to serve the very best homemade ice cream in four flavors—vanilla, chocolate and strawberry, plus a flavor of the day. It had been a favorite spot for the counselors to hang out during their infrequent free time. Adam pulled the BMW to a stop, then turned to Julia. "What would you like?"

She opened the door and hopped out and he quickly followed. "This place hasn't changed at all," she said with a smile. "It's nice to know that some things never change."

He took her hand, weaving his fingers through hers, as they walked up to the window. To an outside observer, they looked like any other couple. Adam liked the way that felt even though the gesture was new to him.

Julia ordered a strawberry cone and he followed up with a chocolate malt. Once he'd paid for their order, they wandered over to a picnic table sitting beneath a sprawling maple tree.

Julia's gaze fixed on his malt as he took a sip through the straw. "What?"

"Are you going to eat that cherry?"

"You want it?" he asked.

"If you're not going to eat it."

"What will you give me for it?" he asked.

A tiny smile twitched at the corners of her mouth. "You want me to pay for it?"

"Or trade," Adam suggested.

"I suppose you want a kiss?"

He shook his head. "I think you can do much better than that. And I don't have to have payment now. You can defer it until later."

She considered his offer silently. Then, as if to challenge him, she ran her finger through her ice cream, then drew it into her mouth. The action was blatantly suggestive and Adam knew that he was probably outmatched in this particular game. All she had to do was smile at him and he got hard.

"You think that deserves a cherry?" he asked.

"You know, I could probably walk up to the window, ask for a cherry and they'd give me one. Maybe even two. For free."

"What fun would that be?" Adam asked with a playful pout.

"I think you're overestimating the value of that cherry."

Grudgingly, he plucked the cherry off the top of his malt and held it out to her. Julia opened her mouth and he dropped it in. But then she grabbed his hand and slowly licked the whipped cream off the tips of his fingers.

A shiver skittered down his spine as he thought about the pleasure she could bring forth with just her lips and her tongue. He drew his hand away, his imagination filled with all the possibilities. "Maybe we should have gotten that motel room," he said.

Julia's brow arched inquisitively. "Let's go," she said.

"Really? You want to do this?"

"I'm sure we could think of an excuse for being late."

"Flat tire," Adam said.

"Lost wallpaper," she added.

"Attacked by bears." He reached out and grabbed her hand, then pulled her along toward the car. Adam wasn't sure what caused the change in her mood, but if it had anything to do with ice cream and cherries, he was going to bring her here more often.

THEY FOUND A room at the Seven Lakes Resort, a beautiful lakeside hotel in the next town that offered all the amenities. But Julia didn't care about the mini-bar or the pool or the gourmet restaurant just off the lobby. She didn't even care about the odd look the clerk gave them both when they checked in without luggage.

All that really mattered was that they'd be completely alone, without fear of being discovered. They'd figure out the excuses later.

After a quick stop at the gift shop, they rode the elevator up to the third floor in silence, his fingers tangled in hers, their eyes fixed on the row of numbers above the doors. The hallway was empty and Julia held her breath as Adam slid the key card into the door.

A moment later, they were inside, the door closed against the outside world. Before she could even take a breath, he grabbed her face between his hands and kissed her. The kiss was frantic and desperate and they stumbled into the room, clutching each other like two people about to drown in a tide of passion.

Julia grabbed the front of his T-shirt and yanked it over his head, needing to feel his bare skin beneath her touch. They couldn't seem to get close enough and they tore at each other's clothes until all they had left was underwear. The feel of his body against hers was exhilarating, like some crazy carnival ride that frightened her and thrilled her all at once.

He slid his hands down along her thighs and clutched her backside, pulling her hips to his. He was aroused and Julia enjoyed the fact that he couldn't seem to control himself when they came together.

"What the hell are you doing to me?" he murmured, his breath warm against her ear.

Emboldened by his reaction, she reached between him and rubbed her hand over his stiff shaft. "The same thing you're doing to me," she replied.

Adam pushed back and looked into her eyes. "Can we just say it out loud? I'm man enough to admit that I want you. More than I've ever wanted a woman in my life. And I think you want me, right?"

"Maybe," Julia murmured.

"Not maybe," he said, shaking his head.

She gave him a grudging smile. "Yes, I want you." She had tried to remain blasé about the prospect of jumping into bed with him, but she couldn't any longer. Every ounce of her being came alive at his touch, every corner of her soul ached for more than just a kiss or a caress.

What if it was the most wonderful experience of her life? What if no other man could ever match what they shared together? Could she handle having the memory of Adam Sutherland stuck in her head for the next fifty or sixty years?

He cut her thoughts off with a long, lingering kiss, one that made her head spin and her body tremble. Julia wanted to stop him, but she'd lost all sense of who or what she was. Every bit of her attention was focused on the taste of his mouth, the feel of his lips against hers.

"Say it then," he whispered, his lips brushing against hers as he spoke.

"I do want you," Julia replied. "I can't seem to help myself."

"I can't either." Adam picked her up and wrapped her legs around his waist, then carried her to the bed. He gently set her down, stretching out above her.

Julia knew the power of his touch on her body. Now, she wanted to test her power over him. She slipped her hand beneath the waistband of his boxers and gently stroked him, wrapping her fingers around his erection. Adam closed his eyes and groaned, his hand tangling in the hair at her nape.

He arched into her touch, and when she looked up again, his eyes were open and he was watching her every move. "I don't think my first time felt this good."

Julia smiled, then tugged his boxers over his hips. He kicked them off and then helped her dispose of the last of her clothes. She wanted to pause for just a second, to take in the sight of his body, the long, muscular limbs, the wide shoulders and flat belly, the smooth chest.

Everything about him was so incredibly male. Though she'd had lovers before, none of them had ever made her feel so womanly, as if her seductive powers were magic only she possessed. Julia felt as if she could surrender by simply closing her eyes and giving herself over to his touch. She was close to climaxing already and they'd barely begun. An urgency drove her forward, toward something she craved.

Adam grabbed her waist and rolled over on top of her, his erection pressing at the juncture of her thighs. "We're going to need a condom," he said.

"Please tell me you came prepared," she murmured.

He reached for his shorts and pulled a foil packet from his wallet.

"You came prepared," she said.

"I jut took care of it. I wasn't going to let any chances slip by, Jules."

She wriggled her fingers and he put the condom in her hand. After she'd carefully sheathed him, Julia straddled his hips, moving above him until he probed at her entrance. Then, with exquisite patience, she sank down on top of him.

The sensation of him filling her was a revelation. It was perfection and paradise, absolute intimacy. They were closer than they'd ever been before and yet, it seemed so natural, as if their bodies had been made for this all along.

Adam began to move inside her, his gaze fixed on hers, his hands tangled in her hair. Julia leaned forward and ran her tongue along the crease of his mouth. He reached out and drew her into a long and sensuous kiss, his lips and tongue communicating his pleasure without words.

Adam reached between them to touch her, but Julia grabbed his hand and pinned it at his side. She was already just a heartbeat away from letting go completely and his touch would send her over. Instead, she increased her tempo, rocking faster and faster and feeling the tension tighten inside of her. She ached for release, but Julia knew that if she waited just a bit longer, it would be all the more intense. She wanted to come, but she wanted it to be the most powerful climax she'd ever experienced.

Adam wasn't content to play a passive role anymore. He sat up and wrapped her legs around his waist, impaling her until she could feel him deep inside of her. When he began to move, she knew she was lost. Every stroke was exquisite torture.

Julia felt herself reaching for ecstasy, her release so close she could almost touch it. And then, it came down on her like a waterfall, crashing over her until her whole body tingled with sensation. She cried out as spasm after spasm shook her, her body reacting uncontrollably.

And then suddenly, Adam was there with her, driving into her one last time before joining her. He pressed his face between her breasts as he moaned, his hands clutching at her shoulders, driving her down onto him again and again until he was completely spent.

When their shudders had subsided, they collapsed back into the bed. Adam gathered her in his arms. It had happened so quickly and yet, Julia felt complete and utter exhaustion. Her body, so tense just moments before, was almost boneless. "Oh, my," she murmured.

"I'll second that," he murmured, pressing a kiss beneath her ear. He raked his hand through her tangled hair, then gently tugged back until she met his gaze. "I can't go the whole week pretending that this never happened. How am I supposed to be around you now? How can I keep from touching you and kissing you?"

"We'll just have to be careful," Julia said. She

stretched out beside him, running her hand over his chest. "We could always rent another room."

"Maybe we should see if this place has a weekly rate," he murmured, pulling her into another long, deep kiss.

They gave themselves another hour in bed and they spent it curled up in each other's arms and talking. Though they hadn't had much time alone to be intimate, they'd had even less to just get to know each other. Before long the subject turned to Mason and Kate.

"I made a call this morning to Grace Winspear," Julia said as she toyed with a lock of Adam's hair.

"Winspear? Like the Chicago Steel Winspears?"

Julia nodded. "She runs the family foundation. I did her daughter's wedding cake last year. I've done three birthday cakes for her grandchildren and an anniversary cake for a party she threw for her sister. And I've helped out with several of her charity events."

"What did she say?" Adam asked, bracing his head on his hand as he looked down at her.

"She said she'd be very interested in receiving a proposal about funding the camp and that I should be sure to send it directly to her so that she can give it her full attention."

Adam smiled. "Do you know what this means? The Winspear Foundation is huge. They fund all sorts of initiatives in Chicago."

"I figured it was big. She spends a lot of money on

cakes. She loves my mandarin orange with white chocolate frosting."

"And the fact that she wants to see a proposal herself is huge! We're going to need to work on it when we
get back to the camp. I want to know everything about
her. We'll have to research the foundation and tailor
the report specifically to their goals." He bent over and
kissed her softly. "You did good."

"Thanks. I made a phone call."

"I know. A very important phone call. Now, I just
need to make sure I do my job."

"Right now, I have another job for you," Julia teased.

"And what would that be?"

"There's a really big shower in that bathroom and I'm
hoping you'll wash my back?"

Adam rolled out of bed and held out his hands. "Do
you think they'd believe it if we told them we had two
flat tires?"

"I'm thinking a flat tire and a dead battery would
work just fine." She chuckled. "As long as we remember to get the wallpaper first."

"No, no, no. You need to move it up. The pattern has to
match. See, it goes bird, flower, leaf, flower. You can't
put two flowers next to each other."

Adam frowned as he stared at the wallpaper. When
he'd volunteered to help Julia wallpaper the small
nurse's office just off the main dining hall, he thought
it would give them another chance to be alone. But Julia

had been determined to focus on work and she'd turned into a tyrant when it came to details.

"What difference does it make?"

"It makes a huge difference. I thought you said you knew how to wallpaper."

"I lied," Adam admitted. "I just wanted to spend some time with you."

She turned around to face him. They'd been struggling in the small space for almost two hours and had managed to finish just one wall. There was paste on almost every inch of his body and his bare feet were sticking to the floor, but he wasn't about to resign his job just yet.

He readjusted the paper. "How's that?"

"Now it's too low on the top. You have to go up two more flowers. There. That's good. Now make sure the seam is straight." She sighed softly, then slipped between him and the wall to show him what she wanted.

He'd always heard that doing home improvements with a woman was a recipe for disaster, but after helping Julia with the screens yesterday, he'd been hopeful that an afternoon in close quarters would be a perfect way to spend more time together. Unfortunately, she took her job very seriously.

"We could have just painted this room and been done with it. Why did it have to be wallpapered?"

"Because Kate wanted it to be cheerful," Julia said.

"I think one wall should be enough. How are we going to do that part around the window?"

"It just takes time," she said. "God, you are so impatient."

He grabbed her around the waist and pressed a kiss to her neck. "Maybe we should take a break," he said. "It's getting really hot in here."

"This is a one-day job," she said. "We have to finish."

"We could take a swim," he suggested. A low rumble of thunder shook the windowpanes and Adam glanced outside. The sky was dark and raindrops streaked the glass. "It's raining. I love swimming in the rain. It's either that or a shower. I have wallpaper paste in places that shouldn't be sticky."

Julia spun around and dragged a finger along the bridge of his nose, leaving a ridge of paste behind. "You didn't have any there," she said.

He reached in the bucket and scooped a glob onto his fingertip, then dropped it in her cleavage. "And you didn't have any there."

With a scream, Julia slapped a handful of paste across his cheek and then ran out of the room. Adam grabbed the bucket and raced after her. They made one circle of the dining hall before she ran out the door and into a downpour. He caught her around the waist and tried to dump the remainder of the paste onto her head, but it ended up on the front of his shirt as they fell into the wet grass.

Breathless with laughter, Julia rolled on top of him, squishing the paste between them both. She turned her face up to the rain and he watched as it fell onto her cheeks and clung to her lashes. At that moment, he couldn't help himself. She looked beautiful…and absolutely irresistible. He kissed her.

At first, she responded, but then he felt her stiffen in his embrace. "Don't," he whispered against her lips. "Just stop and enjoy the moment. No one is watching."

He wanted to feel completely free to follow their desires, like they had in the hotel room. But she rolled away, moving just out of his reach and he felt the loss as if she'd put miles between them.

Frustration surged inside of him. He lay on his back staring up at the gray sky, the raindrops splattering on his face. Though he understood her point, it wasn't easy having such rigid rules between them. There were times when he needed to touch her, just to reassure himself that she was there.

He glanced around and saw that they were the only people outside. "No one is watching," he said.

"I know," she murmured. "We should go back inside before we get hit by lightning."

The rain was coming down in sheets now. Rivers of mud streamed down the driveway and poured off the roof of the dining hall. The heat had been so oppressive that it was a relief to feel the cool breeze blowing in from the north.

"You go," he said as he sat up. "I'll be in shortly."

A flash of lightning streaked across the sky over the lake and a few minutes later a crack of thunder shook the ground. Julia scrambled to her feet and grabbed his hand. "Come in now," she ordered.

But he stood staring out at the lake, his gaze fixed on a motorboat that skimmed across the water toward the shore. "It's all right. Go."

He sat out in the rain, alone, for another few minutes, trying to convince himself that expecting more from Julia would only cause him frustration. Why did he have to push so hard? Why couldn't he be satisfied with what she offered?

In any other situation, a weeklong affair would have been perfect. Just enough time to explore their sexual interests and not enough time to develop any serious expectations. But from the moment he'd found her, cowering with her tennis racquet beside the bed in Woodchuck, he'd been desperate to define their relationship.

Were they just friends? Friends with benefits? Casual lovers? He ran his hands through his wet hair, smoothing it away from his face. Why should it make a difference? What was it about Jules that made him obsess about such inconsequential matters?

Whatever was meant to happen between them would happen. It was just that he'd always been the one in control when it came to romance. Now he felt as if he were hurtling down a mountainside in a car without brakes.

Another flash of lightning split the sky to the west and Adam got to his feet and walked back to the dining hall. Julia was inside standing next to a table near the kitchen. She'd grabbed a few dishtowels and was drying her hair.

The interior of the hall was dark and still, the only sound coming from the rain on the tin roof. Adam walked over to her and she handed him a towel. He grasped her shoulders and gently turned her around, then began to dry her hair, rubbing the damp strands between his hands.

"I love afternoons like this," she said. "It's been so hot lately, it seems like everything is covered in a layer of dust. And then the rain whips up and everything is fresh and clean again."

"I remember it always meant the end to any work. Rainy days were for hanging out in the cabins and relaxing. Long games of chess or Risk or Monopoly."

"Playing old records in the dining hall," she said. "And dancing. I wonder if that old record player is still around."

Adam walked over to a closet near the fireplace where the games were usually kept. He pulled the door open and reached inside to turn on the light. Julia gasped softly, then smiled up at him. All the old familiar things were still there, now neatly stacked on shelves.

"Look at this," he said. "It's like a time capsule. I can't believe they kept all this stuff."

"I can. You know how sentimental Mason is." Julia rummaged around on the bottom shelf and pulled out the old blue record player and a small case that held the 45s. "Here it is."

"I'm not sure kids these days even know what a 45 looks like."

"Hey, you and I grew up with CDs. These records are older than we are."

They sat down on the floor near the closet and Julia began to flip through the records. "Bobby Sherman, David Cassidy. Oh, I remember this one. 'Red Rubber Ball.' I loved that song. And Tommy James's 'I Think We're Alone Now.' Gosh, these all seem so squeaky clean. I guess that's why they kept them."

"Come on, let's put one on." He leaned over and plugged the record player into the wall socket. "It still works."

"'Puppy Love,'" Julia cried. "Donny Osmond. My all-time favorite." She handed the record to him and he slipped it out of the paper sleeve.

"I remember this one," he said. "It was playing at once of the dances we had. You were wearing a green dress with a big black bow around your waist. We were somewhere around fifteen. And you were dancing with David Mitchell."

"You remember that?" she asked.

"Yeah, I remember I wanted to go over and punch him in the face because he kept trying to cop a feel. I thought, if I ever got a chance to dance with you, I'd behave myself."

"I can't believe you remember that."

"You looked so pretty that night. Your hair was curled and you had tied it back in a ribbon. I wanted to ask you to dance. I stood right over there and watched you for most of the night."

"Why didn't you ask?"

"I was afraid you'd say no. You'd turned down Doug O'Neill about five times that night."

"He was a stalker."

"And you didn't like me."

"I would have said yes," Julia insisted.

"Then say yes now," he countered. Adam picked up the record player and carried it to a small table set against the wall. He plugged it in and, to his surprise, it worked. "You choose the song."

With a smile, she slowly rose and held out a record. "It has to be 'Puppy Love,'" she said.

Adam set the needle into place and the music began. The record was badly scratched, but the wavering sound coming from the player's tinny speaker brought back a flood of memories.

He chuckled softly. "Nothing like old vinyl." He stood up and held out his hand. "Dance with me."

Julia shook her head.

"Come on," he teased. "It's just a simple dance. Like when we were kids. Just for fun."

She slowly straightened and he led her out into the middle of the dining hall. The rain still battered the roof, but when he wrapped her arms around his neck, all he heard was the music. "This is how we used to do it, right?"

Julia giggled. "Yes, this is how we used to do it. Make sure you keep your hands on my waist."

They rocked back and forth, like a couple of clumsy kids, following the slow rhythm of the song. Adam began to sing along with the words and though he didn't have much of a voice, it was enough to amuse Julia. "God, this song is sappy," he said.

"I know. But we were kind of sappy back then, too."

The screen door squeaked and they both turned to see Frannie and Ben stumble in, drenched from the rain. For an instant, Adam thought Julia would pull away, but he held tight to her waist.

Frannie's eyes lit up. "Are we having a rainy day dance? Oh, I used to love those." She grabbed Ben's hand and dragged him over to where Adam and Julia stood. "Come on, Benny, show me your moves."

Grudgingly, Ben put his hands on Frannie's waist and they joined in. When the song was over they played it again for Mason and Kate and Steve and Derek, who arrived during a lull in the storm.

And as he held Julia close, Adam realized that he was glad this was their first dance. Such important events should be left for a time when they could be appreciated. "If I ask you to meet me behind the boathouse tonight, will you be there?"

"Is that where you meet all your girls?" Julia said, smiling up at him.

"I don't have any other girls. There's just you."

5

I hate boys! Or maybe I just hate one boy!!! If he only knew I hated him, then maybe hating him would make a difference. But he doesn't know I exist. Last summer, he smiled at me once. And I'm not even sure that was a smile. He might have been laughing at me. This summer, he's so in love with C.P. that all he can think about is her. They're always sneaking off behind the boathouse. Everyone says they're doing it. God, I could just scream. From now on, I hate him.

THEY WERE ALL gathered in the rec hall, bowls of popcorn scattered among them, as they watched a DVD of *The Empire Strikes Back* on the camp's big-screen television. Movie night had replaced the marshmallow roast that Kate had planned when the rain continued on through the evening.

Julia had hoped to ask Kate for the journal, but they hadn't had a chance to talk privately all day long. Once the book was back in her possession, she was sure it would be forgotten. But until that time, she was worried it might reappear for entertainment again.

She stretched her arms over her head and yawned. "I'm heading to bed," she murmured.

"Oh, come on," Kate said. "It's early yet."

"I know. But you're talking to someone who runs a bakery. I'm at work by 4:00 a.m. most mornings. Which means bedtime for me is 8:00 p.m. If I mess up my schedule now, I'll regret it later."

Kate laughed. "Didn't we tell you? We're not letting any of you go home. We're kidnapping you and keeping you all here with us to help run the camp. So you can stay up with us all night long."

"What are you talking about?" Mason asked Kate. "You're usually curled up in bed by nine most nights."

Kate groaned. "Oh, we're getting so old."

Tipping her head, Julia massaged a spot on her neck. "That nurse's room did me in. I'm sore from wallpapering."

"You did a beautiful job," Kate said.

"*We* did a beautiful job," Adam said from his spot at the end of the old leather sofa. "You forget that I was also part of the project. Bird, leaf, flower, leaf. Or something like that."

"Yes, you, too," Mason agreed. "You make a good pair. I think we'll team you up again tomorrow. At least you don't spend half a day arguing like Frannie and Ben."

Frannie grabbed a handful of popcorn and threw it at Mason. "Ben likes it when I boss him around," she said. "Don't you, Benny?"

He grinned. "Yeah, sure, Frannie. And I like it better when you bring the whip and the black leather hot pants." Frannie screamed, then launched herself at Ben, popcorn ammunition in hand.

"I think I'm going to go for a swim," Adam said, getting to his feet. "Come on, Jules, I'll walk you back."

"You shouldn't swim alone," Kate called as they headed to the door.

Adam turned around and held his arms out. "So, who's coming with me? Anyone?"

When there were no takers, Kate waved him off. "Jules, you sit on the end of the pier and watch him, will you? Don't let him swim alone."

Julia nodded and together, they walked out into the damp night air. Once they were out of sight of the rec hall, Adam took her hand and drew it up to his lips, pressing a kiss on the back of her wrist. "See, that wasn't so bad, was it? We're all friends here."

"You know we're not just friends," Julia said.

"So what are we, Ms. McKee?"

She shrugged. "I don't know yet. It's a little too early in our relationship to start planning for the future, don't you think?"

"Well, when you figure it out, will you let me know?" He wrapped his arm around her waist and pulled her closer. "And right after that, we'll let everyone else know, too. Not that they'd even care."

"Oh, they'd care," Julia said. "I know Frannie and Kate would care."

"Do you care that Frannie and Ben are sleeping together?"

Julia gasped. "No! They're not sleeping together. Frannie would have said something. Besides, Ben has a girlfriend."

Adam chuckled. "Didn't you see what was going on all night long? All the flirting, all the teasing. When they weren't wrestling around, they were fetching things from the kitchen together. And Ben keeps his stuff in my cabin, but he didn't sleep there last night."

She considered the notion for a long moment. "Frannie and Ben? They seem like such an unlikely couple. He's so—" Julia stopped herself, then cursed softly. "See, this is what I'm trying to avoid. Now *we're* talking about *them*. We're speculating and making judgments and it's none of our business what they're doing together. This is my point. Once it all becomes public knowledge, then everybody has an opinion. Right now, it's just us."

"Is it?"

Julia stopped short. "I haven't said anything to anyone. Have you?"

He shrugged. "That's not what I'm talking about, Jules. I'm beginning to wonder why it's so important that we keep our relationship under the radar. And I'm thinking that it might be because you have some guy waiting for you back in Chicago."

"You think I have a boyfriend? And I'm cheating on him with you?" She started to laugh, her giggle echoing in the night air. Adam continued to walk toward the lake, ignoring her laughter. Julia ran after him, then grabbed his hand and pulled him to a stop. "Answer me."

"What am I supposed to think?"

"I'm not dating anyone. I'm not. You don't have any idea how far that is from the truth. In fact, I haven't had a date for at least a year." He seemed unconvinced. "You're being ridiculous. And it's no wonder that you were suspicious, since your own behavior has never been ideal."

"You think I cheat?"

"You don't? As I remember, you juggled more than a few girls at the same time at camp."

Adam cursed beneath his breath. "Am I doomed to be punished for my youthful indiscretions for the rest of my life? I was a kid. I was stupid and self-involved."

"I'm not punishing you," Julia corrected.

"Mason was right. Women are like elephants. They have very long memories."

"Oh, I'm sure sweet talk like that is going to get you lots of dates," Julia said. "Were you talking to Mason about us?"

"No. We were discussing women in general. And how ridiculously irrational they were sometimes."

"I'm not irrational. I'm perfectly within my rights to ask that we keep our relationship between the two of us for the moment."

"So you don't have a man in your life back home?"

"No," she said. "And there are no women in your life?"

"No."

"Now that you have the correct information, you don't have anything to worry about," Julia said. She started off toward the lake, this time, with Adam trailing after her.

She reached the dock and strode out to the end, the sound of her footsteps on the weathered wood echoing across the water. He came up behind her, then tugged off his T-shirt and dropped it at his feet. "Is there something wrong with the fact that I like you?" he asked.

"No. But if you like me, then you should respect my feelings on this. It's just too soon."

He reached for his shorts and unzipped them, then skimmed them down over his hips. "I don't think it is. I think we'd have a much nicer time if we didn't always need to watch ourselves so closely." He cursed softly. "Please tell me this is the last time we have to have this argument."

When he hooked his fingers in the waistband of his boxers, she held out her hand to stop him. "Don't do that."

"I'm going swimming. If I want to get naked, I can."

"Oh, and I suppose you think that's going to make me

change my mind?" Julia held her breath as he took his boxers off. Maybe she shouldn't be so difficult. After all, they were among friends.

Before, it was her own insecurities holding her back. But she knew she'd soon have to tell Adam about Paris, about Jean-Paul and about her plans to reboot her life in France. When she'd jumped into this "thing" with Adam, she'd just assumed he'd be happy with a short-term fling, a way to live out a fantasy. It's not like he'd never been one to offer any long-term promises to the other women in his life, at least, not that she knew of.

But now, it was growing more apparent by each minute they spent together, that he had actual plans for their future. Maybe not marriage and happily-ever-after, but certainly a relationship once they got back home. She groaned softly, turning away from the sight of his beautiful body and from the mad rush of desire coursing through hers.

And when he grabbed her arm and spun her around to face him, she didn't have the heart to resist. She wanted to kiss him, wanted to run her hands over his warm skin. Adam pulled her into his embrace and brought his mouth down on hers in a deliberately provocative kiss. His hands strayed to her face and he held her gently as he took everything he wanted and gave her everything she needed.

At first, she was afraid to touch him, knowing that once she started, she wouldn't want to stop. But her hands smoothed over his chest and shoulders, then came to rest on his hips. When he finally pulled back, she felt light-headed and unable to think clearly.

"Take your clothes off, Jules, and come swimming with me." He gave her one last kiss, then stepped to the edge of the dock and dove into the water. His naked body barely made a splash as it split the calm surface. Julia watched, waiting for him to come up. When he didn't, she stepped closer to the edge of the dock.

Another ten seconds passed and he still hadn't come up. A sick feeling knotted her stomach. "Adam?" she called. "Adam, don't mess with me!" She searched the surface for any movement, but in the dark, she could barely see. Had he hit his head when he dove in?

Julia kicked off her sandals, then glanced over her shoulder at the rec hall. By the time she summoned help, it would be too late. "Adam!" She jumped off the end of the dock and an instant later, the cool water hit her body, shocking the breath from her lungs. When she surfaced, she called his name again. But this time he answered.

She saw him swimming about ten feet from her, treading water. "So, you decided to join me?" he called. "Does this mean we're not fighting anymore."

"Where were you?" she screamed. "I thought you'd drowned."

He laughed, kicking back as he stared up at the night sky. "And you jumped in to save me?" Adam swam over to her and grabbed her around the waist. "And you didn't bother to take your clothes off. Hmm."

"I thought something had happened to you," she said,

shoving him away and splashing water in his face. Julia swam to the ladder at the end of the dock and crawled up the steps. "You did that on purpose. You just wanted me to come in with you."

"Come on, Jules. I didn't. I swear. I was just swimming around underwater. I didn't realize I'd been under so long."

She picked up her shoes. "I'm going to bed. I'll see you in the morning."

"You're supposed to stay here and make sure I don't drown," he teased.

Cursing beneath her breath, she turned to walk back up the dock. "I'm sure you can look after yourself."

"Maybe you should go to bed," he yelled. "You're awfully crabby tonight."

She bit back a reply, refusing to be goaded into an argument. Her wet skirt clung to her legs, making it difficult to walk and she stubbed her toe on a loose board at the end of the dock. With an unladylike grunt, Julia hopped to the grassy lawn, then limped alongside the path in the grass.

Sure, the sex was great and it wasn't difficult to spend time looking into a face that handsome. And yes, Adam was smart and charming and funny. But that didn't mean she had to fall all over herself every time he took his clothes off. He was just a guy and sometimes guys were just not worth all the trouble they caused.

ADAM STRETCHED OUT in his bed, his hair still damp from his swim. He'd walked back from the lake alone, his thoughts consumed with the argument he'd had with Julia. It wasn't really an argument but a minor adjustment in their relationship.

It was good that they'd gotten those concerns out in the open. She was far too willing to believe he was still that same shallow guy he'd been at twenty-two. And he was frustrated with her need for secrecy.

With a soft sigh, he grabbed the book beside him on the bed and flipped through the pages of the journal. He scanned the printed entries, searching for details. His attention was caught by a description of C.P. Caroline Perronne? C.P. He'd spent an entire summer chasing her.

Realization slowly dawned. Could he be the romantic object of this story? He put himself into the narrative and it all suddenly made sense. And the writer could be only one person—Julia.

The events she described were things he vaguely remembered. The cake, the dance, the love letter gone astray. She'd fallen in love with him the moment they met and her feelings had continued until the day they'd said good-bye, ten years later.

He closed his eyes and sighed softly. Was this why she'd been so reluctant to make their relationship public? If Kate and Frannie knew about her feelings, wouldn't they have recognized the journal as Julia's?

Was it any wonder she couldn't trust him? From her point of view, he'd never even noticed her in all those years. Instead, his attention had been focused on what appeared to be an endless string of girls who were pret-

tier, blonder, more well-endowed and more sexually pro-
miscuous than she had been.

And never, in her wildest imagination, would she
have believed that he found her as enigmatically attractive as she had found him. He chuckled softly. Maybe it
was better they'd never hooked up all those years ago.
Back then, he probably would have blown any chance he
had with her. But now, he had experience in his corner.

A soft knock sounded on the screen door. Adam sat
up on the edge of the bed, then shoved the journal beneath the mattress. He walked to the door and found
Julia waiting on the other side. She'd changed out of her
wet clothes and was wearing a faded hoodie and shorts.

"Hi," she murmured.

"Hi." He pushed open the door and she slipped inside.
As she passed, he caught hold of her hand and wove his
fingers through hers, turning her around to face him.

"I wanted to apologize for what I said earlier. And
for what I didn't say." She turned her gaze up to meet
his. "I like you. A lot. And I understand your frustration and I don't want to force you to behave in any way
that you find uncomfortable. I'm just dealing with some
things that really shouldn't make a difference, but—"

"Are you breaking up with me?" he asked, not sure
where the conversation was headed.

She blinked, clearly taken aback by his question.
"Are we…" She laughed softly, then shrugged. "I don't
know what to call it. Are we…together?"

"Yes," he said.

"Then, no. We're not breaking up. I'm telling you that if you think it's important to let everyone know what's happening, then go ahead. I don't care."

Adam knew how much it took for her to surrender. And it broke his heart that he hadn't been able to understand the depth of her insecurities before. This was his fault and he needed to make it right.

"No," he murmured, reaching out to smooth a damp strand of her hair from her face. "You were right, Jules. I was just being a jerk."

"No, I think maybe you were right."

He brushed a kiss across her lips. "I think you need to know something about me. When it comes to romance, I'm rarely right. I don't know what the hell I'm doing. I think I do, but then I realize, if I actually did, I'd be happily married by now. Trust me on this, Jules." He brought her hand up to his lips and kissed the inside of her wrist. As his lips rested on her skin, he felt her pulse quicken.

A moment later, her arms slipped around his neck and their mouths met in a long, languid kiss. Relief washed over him as his hands skimmed over her body, naked beneath the hoodie she wore. It wasn't finished. The need for him still burned inside her. With a soft sigh, he picked her up off her feet and his arms wrapped around her waist.

"Tell me that you want me," he whispered, his lips brushing against hers as he spoke.

"I do," Julia replied. "I can't seem to help myself."

"I can't either." Adam carried her to the bed. He gently set her down and they both fell onto the mattress. He was already hard, his cock pressing against the fabric of his boxers.

He'd always wondered what it would be like to make love to her and now that he'd enjoyed the pleasures of her body, it wasn't nearly enough. Like some insidious drug, the experience had only left him wanting more—a desperate need that he couldn't fill with just a kiss or a caress.

He tugged her shirt over her head, then found a spot beneath her breast, a perfect place for his lips and tongue to begin. As he traced a path upward, she arched against him, her fingers tangled in his hair. When both nipples were hard and damp from his tongue, he moved lower, tugging her shorts down over her hips before he found the spot between her legs.

His only thought was to completely possess her, to make it impossible for her to want anyone but him, now and forever. As he teased at the crease between her legs, Adam felt her body begin to tremble. Julia sucked in a sharp breath, then moaned. He stopped, knowing that she was so close she might not be able to help herself. But when she relaxed, he began again. And each time he felt her move toward the edge, he stopped.

Though Adam had always been more than adept in the bedroom, he needed to prove to Julia that the passion between them wasn't just about sex. It was about trust and communication. And about feelings that still remained unspoken between them.

He brought her close again and again, until she was writhing on the bed. And when he finally slipped inside of her, the thin sheath of latex the only thing between them, every nerve in his body was on fire. Determined to maintain control, he moved slowly at first, his mind fixed on the taste of her mouth and not the wild sensations coursing through his body.

His release hit him like an electric shock. Instinct took over and Adam grasped her hips, every conscious thought focused only on the rush of ecstasy that washed over him. And when he felt her body shudder beneath his, Adam let go and dissolved beneath the waves of pleasure.

When he finally drifted back to the real world, he pressed his lips to her forehead, waiting for his breath to slow and his heart to cease hammering in his chest. They were both covered with a sheen of perspiration, the scent of the lake in their hair.

Julia nuzzled against his cheek and sighed softly. They'd made love twice now and both times it was utter perfection, beyond anything he'd ever experienced before. Was this what it felt like, to find the right woman, to fall in love so deeply and inexplicably that there were no words to express it?

"As much as I like arguing with you, Jules, I like this a whole lot better," he whispered.

She laughed softly. "I like arguing with you."

"Why?"

"I feel like I'm getting to know the real you. The guy inside who doesn't always act perfect or look perfect. I like that guy."

Adam pressed his lips to the top of her head, drawing her naked body closer to his. "But I don't want to fight with you anymore. I just want to spend the rest of this week like this, close and quiet. Just the two of us."

She pushed up on her elbow. "It's not really fighting, you know," she said.

"But every time we're at odds, I'm afraid all of this will end. That you'll get mad and get in your car and go home and I'll never see you again."

"No," she said. "I'm not that fragile. But, I don't think we should expect to agree on everything. If you're acting like a jerk, I'm going to tell you."

"And if you're acting like a..."

"A shrew? Well, then you can tell me. Although, I think shrew is a bit harsh. Maybe harpy would be better?" She paused. "No, that's not good either."

"How about crazy woman?"

She met his gaze, then shrugged. "I guess that will do."

"I think maybe it's time to put the past behind us, Jules. We were different people back then. If we keep going there for reference points, we're only going to ruin what we have here."

She nodded. "I know that sounds logical. But sometimes, when I'm with you, I still feel like that teenager.

Like I've never done this before, and it's the most frightening, yet exhilarating thing in the world."

"Me, too," he murmured, dropping a kiss on her lips. She'd just described his idea of what falling in love was like. Maybe that's what was happening here, he mused.

He pulled her body close again, wondering at how perfectly she fit into his arms. "So, can I talk you into staying the night?" he asked.

"I think I can be persuaded."

"You're not afraid someone is going to discover us?"

She snuggled closer. "No. I'm pretty sure I can deal with it."

JULIA WOKE UP in her own bed in Woodchuck, her naked body curled beneath the faded quilt and brand-new sheets. As she opened her eyes to the morning light, she expected to find Adam lying beside her. But the other side of the bed was empty.

She sat up, rubbing her eyes, and wondering if she'd simply dreamed the previous night. But as her mind cleared, she began to recall all the details. They'd started in his cabin, then walked back to hers in the hours after midnight. He'd spent the rest of the night in her bed, making love to her until just before dawn.

She smiled and stretched her arms above her head. It had been a perfect night, a night she'd never forget. And though her body was still exhausted, she was anxious to see him again, to look into his eyes and share a smile.

As Julia pulled on a simple sundress and searched for her sandals, she wondered if she'd walk into a dining hall filled with curious stares and barely concealed smiles. Had he planned to tell everyone about the two of them? Or had Adam left her cabin to preserve their secrets?

She grabbed her cell phone and checked the time. It was close to ten in morning. She noticed a missed call from Grace Winspear's office made an hour before. Plopping down on the center of the bed, she quickly re-dialed the number. "Mrs. Winspear, please," she said when the receptionist answered.

"Mrs. Winspear is out of the office," her secretary explained.

"Can you let her know that Julia McKee returned her call?"

"Miss McKee. Yes. Actually, Mrs. Winspear would like some additional information from you regarding your summer camp project. I have it outlined, but I don't have an email address or a fax number."

Julia quickly gave the secretary her email address, then thanked her. "Let Mrs. Winspear know I'll get back to her first thing tomorrow."

She hung up the phone and jumped off the bed, anxious to tell Adam her good news. If they could get funding for the camp through the Winspear Founda-tion, Mason and Kate could do the kind of work they'd always dreamed of doing.

She found her shoes next to one of the bunks and slipped them on, then quickly ran down to the dining hall. When she stepped inside, she found Kate and Frannie sitting at a table with a sewing machine and a pile of fabric.

They looked up at her as she approached. "Oh, thank God the arts and crafts person is here," Frannie said. "You picked the wrong day to sleep in. I hope you know how to use a sewing machine."

Julia pulled out a chair and sat down. "I do. If I'm not mistaken that's the old machine that was in the rec hall."

"I'm trying to figure out how to thread it," Kate said. "I kind of remember this from camp, but not really."

"What are you making?"

"Curtains," she said. "For the showers. They're just a width of this fabric with a pocket for the rod on one end and a hem on the other three sides. It's not that complicated."

"Why didn't you just buy regular shower curtains?" Julia asked.

"They're expensive and I found all this fabric in a box. I figure if these last for a summer, I'll be happy. At least they're free."

Julia nodded. She could sense the tension in Kate's voice. Though she and Mason tried to stay optimistic about the financial side of the business, it was obvious that there were times when frustration and worry prevailed. "Move," she said, "I'll get it started. You two measure out the fabric to the right length then add a half inch for the bottom and sides and three inches for the top."

Kate stood up to get out of the way, then froze, her eyes going wide. "What is that on your neck?" she asked.

"What?" Julia asked. She brushed her hand beneath her ear. "Is it a bug? A spider? Get it off!"

Frannie stood up. "That...oh my, God, is that a hickey?"

"What?" Julia clapped her palms around her neck.

"Let me see," she cried, prying at Julia's fingers. "Who are you messing around with?"

"Is it Ben? Are you and Ben messing around?" Kate asked.

"No!" Frannie answered at the same time as Julia and they both looked at her.

A blush rose in Frannie's cheeks. "All right. I'm messing around with Ben. Don't look at me like that. He's cute, he's geographically available, he just broke up with a horrible woman and it was a long ride from Minneapolis." Frannie looked at Julia. "So there's only one choice left. Unless you're having a hot and heavy affair with Bigfoot."

"Adam?" Kate gasped. "You and Adam are—"

"Why is that so hard to believe?" Julia asked. "Is it impossible to consider that he might find me attractive?"

"Of course not," Frannie said. "It's just that you hate Adam."

"I don't. I've never hated him. I just never trusted him. But we're both grown ups-and—" She drew a deep breath. "I don't really know what we're doing. I guess I was curious to see what all the fuss was about."

"And?" Frannie asked.

"Are you asking for details? Because if I have to give details, then I think you better be prepared to do the same."

"Yeah," Kate said. "Let's get to the details. Jules first. Then Frannie."

Julia wasn't sure how much she should reveal. Frannie and Kate were her best friends, but she hadn't exactly worked out a logical explanation for her behavior. She'd never told them about her crush, never let on that she'd been in love with Adam since she was twelve. But maybe it was time to let that secret go, too.

"First of all," Julia began. "I never hated Adam. In fact, it was just the opposite. I—"

"It was you," Kate interrupted. "The book. The journal we found in Woodchuck. It was about you and Adam, wasn't it?"

Julia covered her face with her hands. "Yes. And I'd appreciate it if you wouldn't haul that thing out again for breakfast entertainment."

"So you've been in love with Adam all this time?"

"No! I had a crush on him when I was younger. He was the cutest boy in camp. And I think I was just working through all the issues I had with my parents' divorce. It was safe to love him from afar. If it wasn't real, then he couldn't hurt me. So, I carried on this long fantasy. But once I left camp, I barely thought of him."

"And how do you feel about him now?" Frannie asked.

"I don't know. I'm...happy. And a little infatuated. *And* I'm supposed to move to Paris in two months. You know how Adam is. He'll be moving on to his next conquest before long."

"You're supposed to move to Paris?" Frannie smiled. "That isn't the same as you are *going* to move to Paris. Are you thinking of changing your plans?"

Kate leaned forward. "What did he say when you told him you were leaving?"

"I haven't told him—yet. At first, it didn't make a difference. And then, things just started moving so fast that now, I'm afraid if I tell him, he'll be...upset."

"You told him about the journal, though. About your crush."

Julia shook her head. "I haven't told him about that either."

Frowning, Kate sat back in her chair. "Well, he must suspect something because he came and got the book."

"You gave it to him?"

"I didn't know it was yours," Kate said. "Or that it was about him. What difference does it make? You were just a kid. It was a silly crush."

"I know it seems silly, but you know how he is. Adam has always loved the chase. Once he knows he has a girl, he loses interest."

Kate reached out and grabbed Julia's hand. "He has grown up a bit in the past eight years."

"I know," Julia murmured. "I'd like to believe that. But a man like him isn't supposed to end up with a woman like me."

Frannie gasped. "What is that supposed to mean? He'd be lucky to have you."

"I just always imagined that he'd marry someone rich and glamorous, you know, someone his family would approve of. I make desserts for a living. I drive a ten-year-old car and live in a one-bedroom flat that barely has heat in the winter. And I have no idea what I'm doing with this man."

"Well, I think you should tell him," Kate said. "Just put it all out there. Complete and utter honesty. I think it would be wrong to underestimate his feelings for you, Jules."

Julia took a deep breath, straightening her shoulders. After last night, after the quiet intimacies and the whispered affections, maybe it was the right time to tell him everything.

"Is it all right if I do this sewing later? I should really go find him."

"Go on," Kate said. "I think he and Mason are painting the tennis courts."

She pushed her chair back and stood, but the sound of a scream drew her attention to the door.

"Oh, my God, is that Julia McKee?"

Julia watched as a stunning blonde burst through the door of the dining hall. She was dressed in a tailored linen suit that revealed a remarkable amount of cleavage and leg. Her skin was deeply tanned and her fingers perfectly manicured. She looked like she'd just stepped out of a beauty salon, her hair perfectly styled to look sexy, but smart.

Adam stood behind her, lingering in the doorway, watching the scene play out with a mildly curious expression.

"Don't you remember me?" she asked. "And Frannie, is that you? Oh, you two haven't changed a bit."

"Hello, Caroline," Kate said.

Julia's stomach did a back flip. "Caroline Perronne?"

"Yes! Mason mentioned that a bunch of people were coming back for the week to help fix this place up." She turned and grabbed Adam's arm, drawing him into the conversation. "Imagine my surprise to find Adam here. We haven't seen each other in ages."

Julia forced a smile. "And what are you doing here?" The question wasn't phrased perfectly, but all Julia could think about was the way Caroline was hanging on to Adam's arm. Possessively, as if she'd already staked her claim.

"Well, I was the listing agent who sold this place to Mason and Kate. I have my own real estate business in town."

"Oh, right," Frannie interjected. "I forgot you were a townie."

"Yes, some of us get to live here in paradise, while others toil away in the city. Listen, I have a fabulous house on Deacon Lake. You'll all have to come for dinner tonight. Adam said Derek and Steve are here, too."

"They're leaving this afternoon," Kate said.

"Well, then everyone else."

"Oh, I don't think that would be possible," Kate said. "We're far too busy with the camp."

"Nonsense. You can afford to take a few hours off. And I've become quite a cook. Everyone says I should open my own restaurant, but it's impossible to make money at that."

"Yes. Making a lot of money is the most important thing," Adam said.

"Yes," she said, smiling up at him. "I can see you and I are going to have to talk." She put on a bright smile. "So, I will see you all later. Seven? Oh, we'll have fun catching up, won't we?" She wrapped her arms more tightly around Adam's. "Walk me to my car?" she cooed. "You and I have some catching up to do, too."

"Sure," Adam said.

Julia watched as he walked out with Caroline draped on his arm. When the door slammed behind them, she let out a tightly held breath. "Everything that I said about Adam and me? Just forget it all."

Kate frowned. "Come on, Jules, I don't—"

Julia held up her hand to her forehead, sending her friends a wry smile. "I think I feel a migraine coming on. Make sure to give Caroline my regrets, won't you?"

6

I turned eighteen a month ago and graduated from high school two weeks ago. I'm an adult now, at least in the eyes of our government. And yet, I'm still waiting... hoping...wondering if I'm ever going to know what it's like to be with a man. No one seems to be very interested in finding out who I am, least of all the one guy who I really think I could love. Sometimes, I wish I could stay a kid forever. Life was so easy back then.

JULIA BENT OVER the sewing machine, lining up the hem of the shower curtain. The machine clattered as it ate up the length of fabric. When she finished, she glanced over at the clock on the wall. It was nearly eight and she wondered how the dinner party at Caroline's was going.

Both Kate and Frannie had tried to convince her to change her mind, but there was no way she was going to endure an evening of watching Caroline and Adam, the reunion show. According to Kate, the recently divorced

Caroline was on the prowl for the next Mr. Perronne. Was it any wonder she had her sights set on Adam?

"So why do I care?" Julia muttered.

She'd been trying to answer that question all day long. Why did it bother her so much? Was she jealous? If Adam *did* move from her to Caroline, then good riddance. A man who wanted a woman like Caroline wasn't a man that she needed. It wasn't logical to be jealous anyway.

Yet all those same feelings from years ago had been churned up. She tried to ignore them, but they didn't want to go away. Her confidence around men had never been very solid, but now that it had been tested, she realized that she couldn't blame anyone but herself.

She turned back to the sewing machine, determined to finish the project. But her mind wandered again and again, back to Adam and what they'd shared over the past few days. It had all happened so fast that she'd been reluctant to believe it was all real. And yet, the emotions inside of her were crying out to be acknowledged.

She was falling in love with him. That was the only explanation. And it didn't matter what their friends thought or what Caroline Perronne did. Nothing about those feelings could be diminished in the least.

Julia groaned softly, shoving back from the table and covering her face with her hands. She'd tried so hard to stop this from happening. And yet, it snuck up on her, without any warning. Or maybe it had never stopped, not from that very first moment she'd seen him walking across the dining hall eighteen years ago in his Teenage Mutant Ninja T-shirt.

"Are you going to hide out in here all night or are you going to help me with the proposal for Mrs. Winspear?"

Julia peeked through her fingers to find Adam standing on the other side of the table.

"I have all the questions answered," he continued. "I thought maybe you could proof the proposal before I send it?"

"I thought you were going to Caroline's place for dinner."

Adam shrugged. "I made my apologies and told her that I had important work to do."

"You did?"

"And important people to be with," he added.

"You said that to her?"

"No. But I was thinking it. Jules, I'd rather spend a hundred nights watching you paint your toenails than spend a single night with her. You must know that, don't you?"

"Well, no. But now that you said it, I do." She felt her cheeks warm with a blush and she couldn't help but smile at him.

He slowly circled the table, then reached out for her hand, pulling her to her feet the moment he captured it. "We have the whole camp to ourselves," he murmured. "What are we going to do with it?"

"I thought you wanted me to proofread your proposal," she said, brushing the hair out of his eyes.

"That can wait until later."

Julia slowly worked at the buttons of his shirt, then brushed it off his shoulders. His muscled chest was cast in stark shadows from the lights overhead. She ran her hands from his collarbone to his belly, then lower. Her fingertips skimmed across the front of his shorts, feeling his hard shaft pushing against the faded fabric.

When he was with her, it never took much for Adam to get aroused. Julia had never had that power with a man before. There was a certain satisfaction in knowing that she could have Adam whenever she wanted him, that he would be there, ready and willing to satisfy her every need.

She unzipped his shorts and Adam moaned softly as she wrapped her fingers around his heat. Already, his body was so familiar to her. She knew how he'd react to her touch, the way his breath would catch in his throat, the sound of his voice whispering her name.

Adam grabbed her waist and slowly backed her up against the edge of the table. He kissed the curve of her neck and then moved lower, opening the front of her dress to reveal her lacy bra.

Julia braced her hands behind her and watched as he tugged aside the satin and lace to tease at her nipple with his lips and tongue. "Maybe we should go back to your cabin," he suggested as he gently nuzzled her breast.

"Or maybe we should stay here," she said.

He dropped his hand to the soft curve of her backside and gently squeezed. "Maybe?"

"It's a long walk and we're alone."

Adam straightened, his lips finding hers, kissing her gently at first and then with growing urgency, dragging his tongue along the crease of her mouth until she surrendered completely. He pushed her back to lie on the table, her body at the mercy of his touch.

Adam slowly trailed kisses over her shoulder and down her arm. When he knelt in front of her, Julia raked her fingers through his hair, pulling him away when his tongue tickled.

He was so beautiful, so incredibly sexy. She couldn't imagine ever feeling this attracted to a man again. There seemed to be electricity that crackled between them every time they were together. Just one touch of his fingers to her bare skin was all it took for the attraction to overwhelm them both.

"I need you," he murmured. "I need to fall asleep with you in my arms and wake up the same way."

Julia understood how he felt. The luxury of spending an entire night together in bed was one they hadn't yet experienced. "I want that, too," she murmured.

"Then you don't care who knows?"

"Well, Frannie and Kate already know. I told them this afternoon. And you were right about Frannie and Ben."

"It doesn't make a difference, does it."

"It was never about them," Julia admitted. "It was

about me. I just—" She drew a ragged breath. "I wasn't—"

He kissed her belly, wrapping his arms around her waist. "Tell me. You can say anything to me."

"If other people knew, then this suddenly became real. And if it was real, then either it was going to end or it was going to go on. And I just wasn't sure I could handle either of those two possibilities."

"It doesn't have to end," Adam said.

"But it might," she said. "Still, if that's the risk I have to take, then I'm willing to take it. I'm stepping out of the fantasy and into reality."

Adam's kisses trailed lower, until he found the dampness between her legs. She was already aroused and the moment he touched her there, her body jerked in response. "Then there's nothing left to stop us." He gently parted her legs, pulling her panties aside and tasting her until she writhed against him.

"Oh," she breathed. "Oh, right there."

As he brought her closer and closer to her release, Julia murmured his name urgently. Adam followed her cues, dragging her back from the edge when she got too close. It was a game he was starting to enjoy, waiting until she was wild with desire before finally allowing her release.

She reached out and tangled her fingers in his hair, tugging until he looked up at her. He knew what she wanted without her even needing to tell him and when he moved to retrieve a condom from his pocket, Julia grabbed his hand and shook her head. "It's all right," she said. "You don't have to worry."

"Are you sure?"

Julia nodded. She'd been on the Pill for years—it had always seemed like a practical thing. But now, it was liberating. She trusted Adam and he trusted her. She wanted to experience him without any barriers between them. And if they only had a few more nights together, this chance to possess each other completely, then it would be enough. Julia didn't care what came later as long as this came now.

She gently guided him to her entrance and Adam closed his eyes the moment they touched. Slowly, exquisitely, he pushed inside of her. Julia felt the muscles in his body tense, but he didn't give in. Instead, he slowly began to move.

She closed her eyes as well, focusing on the sensations that washed over her body. She was already so close, but this seemed to take her to a higher level, the need growing more intense with each stroke. This was paradise, she thought. There was nothing more perfect.

"I want you," he murmured. "Come for me."

He increased his pace and Julia felt herself dancing on the edge. And when it came, it came so fast that it caught her by surprise. She cried out and the pleasure shook her body, stealing her ability to think.

It was enough to send him over the edge and Adam joined her a moment later. It was simple, uncomplicated and pure, the two of them searching for release and finding it with each other.

He was like an addiction, a craving she could only satisfy for a short time. Though she felt sated now, Julia knew she'd want more. He collapsed beside her, both of them still partially dressed.

Adam pressed a kiss into the curve of her neck. "Can we stay here forever?" he murmured.

"I think this kind of activity isn't what they were thinking about when they built the activity hall," Julia joked.

Adam pushed up on his elbow. "You're supposed to say yes," he teased. "Or I'll feel as if you weren't well satisfied."

"I was," she said.

They lay together, wrapped in each other's arms, for a long time. Julia listened to his breathing. He wasn't asleep and she wondered what he was thinking. But she was afraid to ask. They'd so carefully avoided the subject of the future, but it was coming at them quickly.

"I don't think there's another man on the planet who wants a woman the way I want you," Adam murmured.

"Don't you wonder?" Julia said. "Is this unusual? Are we an...aberration?"

Adam answered before he even considered her question. "This is the way it was meant to be with us," he said.

"What are we going to do when this is over?"

The question took him by surprise and this time, he

didn't have a quick and easy answer. "I don't intend for it be over. Ever."

She drew a ragged breath. He couldn't have made his intentions any clearer. And now, maybe it was time she told him about Paris. She closed her eyes and tried to put her thoughts in order, tried to find a way to broach the subject. But she'd waited too long. She should have told him long before he started thinking about a future together.

"We can't be together forever. We both have careers and responsibilities."

"You have a bakery in Chicago. Unless that blows out of town on the next windy day, I think we're going to be all right."

"What about you? Don't you travel for business?"

"Sure. But I'm usually not gone for more than a week at most." He pressed a kiss to her shoulder. "We don't have to make any plans right now. Except for the night we get back. I'm taking you out to dinner Friday night."

"I can't. I'll have things to do at the bakery. We usually work through the night on Friday because most weddings are on a Saturday."

"All right, then Saturday night," he said.

"I'm usually exhausted. I wouldn't be very good company. And I have to be up early on Sunday for the morning rush at the bakery."

"Sunday night?"

Julia nodded. "The bakery isn't open on Monday. Sunday night would be good."

"Good," he said, grinning. "It's a date. You and me. Dinner, Sunday night."

"I've also been thinking about a trip to Paris," she said. "It's kind of up in the air right now."

"A vacation?"

"More like a professional trip," she said. "To study pastry-making."

"Well, if you're going to Paris, then I'll come with you. I can see some of the sights while you're taking your classes."

Julia snuggled up against his body, pressing her face into his warm skin. That was enough for now, she thought to herself. Let him think it was a week or two of "classes." She didn't need to explain that an apprenticeship would be at least a year's commitment and probably two. Or that this was a chance that anyone in her position would jump at. Or that she was simply keeping her options open, in case things didn't work out with him.

She'd figure all of that out later.

"WELL, THAT DIDN'T go as well as planned," Mason muttered. He pushed open the front door of the bank and stepped out onto the street. With a soft curse, he unknotted his tie. "I don't understand. We're not asking for that much. Just enough to finish the big projects and buy supplies." He started off down the sidewalk toward Adam's car. "Kate is going to freak."

Adam caught up with Mason in a few long strides. "Financing is really tight these days."

"Well, why would they give us the loan to buy the camp and not give us the money to fix it up?"

"Maybe because they're hoping you'll fail?"

Mason snapped his head around. "That doesn't make sense."

"Think about it," Adam said. "You're sitting on land that is worth at least three million and you paid half that. Yet it would be worth triple that if you could build houses or a resort on it. But you can't do that. At least, not yet. If you're forced to sell, then the agreement requiring you to maintain the camp could be challenged in court. The bank could repossess the camp if you get behind and they'd be sitting on a goldmine. If you sell it outright, they have a shot to finance whatever the new buyer decides to do."

"Jesus," Mason muttered. "You really think that's what's going on here?"

"Yeah, Mase, I do. They're hedging their bets. If they lend you more, you might actually make a go of it. They'd rather you failed and the faster the better."

"We can't fail. My parents, Kate's parents, they've put some of their money into this. Kate took money from her grandmother. We've got close to a million invested already."

"I know. I've seen the figures."

"I can't ask my family—or Kate's—for any more money."

"You can ask me," Adam said. "I'll invest."

"No. I couldn't ask you to do that."

"What if I wanted to do it?" Adam asked. "I want to see Winnehawkee back up and running as much as you do."

"We're going to make it work. We just have to find another way. I mean, if we need to go back to aiming the camp at overprivileged kids, then I guess we'll do that. We had an offer to lease the entire thing out to the YMCA which I suppose we could reconsider as well."

"Not quite yet," Adam said. "There are a few more possibilities that I'm working on right now. You'll just need to be patient for a bit longer."

"How can I be patient when all of this is hanging over our heads?"

Adam clapped his hand on Mason's shoulder. "Don't worry about it yet. I'm on the job. And so is Jules."

"Jules? What is she doing?"

"She knows some very influential people in Chicago, especially one particular philanthropist who runs a foundation that funds programs like this."

Mason sighed softly, shaking his head. "You guys have already done so much."

"I told you I'd help with this and I meant it."

Mason leaned back against the car, his shoulders slumped. "Have I just made the biggest mistake of my life?"

"No. You're all right for now. But, I think it might be a good idea to enlist some more support, especially with the locals. As annoying as she is, Caroline Perronne would be someone to have in your corner. She seems to have a lot of power in this town. I think you might want to consider naming her to your board of directors."

"I was going to name you to the board of directors," Mason said.

"All the more reason that Caroline will want to join as well."

"You know, you could have brought this up with Caroline last night at dinner. But wait! You didn't go to dinner with us last night."

"I had some other things I needed to take care of," he said.

"I think you'd be the perfect candidate to charm Caroline Perronne into helping us," Mason suggested.

Adam slowly shook his head. "Charm or seduce? Because I have my limits and they pretty much stop at charm."

"Kate says that you and Jules are an item."

He laughed. "Is that what she says? I guess she'd know. Probably better than I do, at this point. Julia hasn't been very forthcoming with her feelings for me."

"You haven't…"

"Oh, we have. And the physical stuff is amazing. We just haven't locked down the romantic, happily-ever-after stuff."

"And how do you feel?"

Adam stopped walking, not sure how to answer that question. "I feel optimistic. I'm happy. Really happy for the first time in—probably since I graduated from college. I think I'm in love with her."

"You know what? That deserves a beer. It's past noon. There's a tavern on the corner. Let's celebrate your good fortune. At least one of us knows what the future holds."

"Well, I wouldn't go that far." Adam said.

"So, how do you think she's going to react to you charming Caroline for me? Because all that woman did last night at dinner was talk about you."

Adam grabbed the door of the pub and held it open for Mason. "I think she'd understand that it's for a good cause." He shook his head. "At least I hope that's what she'll think."

In truth, Julia would probably support whatever had to be done to be sure Mason and Kate made a success of the camp. "I suppose I could meet Caroline for dinner. Or lunch. Lunch is in the middle of the day. Breakfast would probably be perfect. She'd have to leave and get to work. There'd be no expectations. And no alcohol involved." He groaned. "Somehow, I'm getting the feeling that this plan has disaster written all over it."

Mason walked through the bar and sat down on a stool, Adam taking the spot next to him. "Think about it."

"Right," Adam murmured.

A week ago, Adam wouldn't have thought twice about it. Anything to help Mason, even if it involved seducing a former girlfriend. But now, he had something to lose—something he wasn't willing to risk. Intimacy wasn't just about the physical anymore. He'd experienced a revelation with Julia, a realization that great sex wasn't the only thing he craved from a woman.

Adam loved the affection, the simple, quiet moments between them, the shared secrets, the warm laughter, the knowledge that she didn't want to be with any other man on the planet but him. They were a pair, two people who had found each other against all odds.

He dreaded spending a single minute with Caroline. A minute with her was a minute away from Julia. "I'll mention it to Jules and see what she thinks," he murmured.

"Oh, man, you are in love, aren't you."

The bartender set their beers in front of them and Mason picked his up, taking a long swig. "So what am I going to tell Kate about the bank? How am I going to explain this to her?"

"Wait," Adam advised. "Tell her they haven't made a decision yet. They need more paperwork from me. Let's see what happens with the Winspear Foundation. And I've got a few other things that might work out as well."

"We've got enough to make it through the winter. But we have to get paying campers for three solid months next summer or we'll be in trouble." He stared into his beer. "Sometimes I wonder if chasing a dream like this is just an exercise in futility."

"No," Adam said. "If you have a dream, you have to go for it. You only have one life, Mase, and it doesn't pay to live it with regrets. If you want something, you go after it, no holds barred."

Adam took a sip of his beer. Maybe he should be taking some of his own advice. He'd managed to stumble into his dream and now he had to find a way to keep it from disappearing in front of his eyes.

"ARE WE HAVING fun yet?" Kate leaned over Julia and handed her a glass of lemonade, spiked liberally with vodka.

"Oh, we're having a lovely time," Julia muttered, staring across at Caroline Perronne.

The beautiful blonde was sitting next to Adam, perched on a long log. The boys had built a campfire and dinner had been hot dogs, campfire potatoes cooked in tin foil and a dessert of toasted marshmallows.

Uninvited, Caroline had appeared unexpectedly right before the dessert course and had slipped into Julia's place while Julia was in the kitchen with Kate. Since then, she'd monopolized Adam's attention, engaging him in private conversation, finding any excuse to touch him, laughing at everything he said.

Though Adam had explained the importance of courting Caroline's favor, it didn't make it any easier to watch. Julia felt as if she'd been transported back to her teenage years once again, forced to observe from the shadows while the object of her affection turned his attentions to someone she considered completely unworthy.

Adam was friendly, but not nearly as interested as he had been years ago. The only delight Julia found in the situation this evening was that Caroline seemed to be plagued by mosquitoes. The more she drank, the more they seemed to bother her. She'd taken to slapping at them in frustration, rubbing her bare legs and tugging at her tiny sundress as much as she could.

"How long do you think she'll last?" Frannie murmured.

"Not much longer," Kate replied. "I expect she's waiting for the right moment to drag him off to some private spot and have her way with him."

"I wonder why the mosquitoes just won't leave you alone, Caroline. They're not really bothering anyone else," Julia said in a deceptively sweet voice.

"It must be my perfume," she said in an annoyed tone, slapping her cheek.

Julia picked up the repellant and tossed the tube over the campfire. "I'm sure Adam could help you put some of that on. Adam, rub a little bit of that on Caroline, won't you?"

Julia could see Caroline's mind working as she examined the tube. Was the prospect of Adam smoothing lotion on her skin more attractive than the smell of the lotion was repellant? "Oh, no, this stuff is horrid. It smells awful. And it's just horrible for the skin."

"Well, maybe Adam can take you out for a canoe ride," Julia suggested. "The mosquitoes aren't usually too bad out on the water. Adam loves taking the canoe out at night, don't you, Adam?"

He sent her a disapproving look and she smiled sweetly. "In fact, the last ride we took was quite lovely."

"Oh, yes, let's get out of here," Caroline said, popping up from her spot. She grabbed Adam's hand. "Look, the moon is just rising. It will be so—"

"Romantic!" Julia cried. "Oh, yes. Very romantic."

"Would you like to come with us, Jules?" Adam asked. "There's room in the canoe for three."

"No, she's fine right where she is," Caroline said. "She said the mosquitoes aren't bothering her."

Julia watched as they walked off into the darkness, Caroline pulling Adam along by the hand. He glanced back at Julia once and Julia waved at him.

"Mason, this is a bad idea," Kate muttered. "Who knows what she's going to try once she has him alone?"

"Adam can take care of himself," Mason replied.

"And you!" Kate cried, turning her attention to Julia. "What were you thinking?"

"I got tired of watching Caroline drooling all over him," Julia said. "We weren't going to get rid of her without him."

Frannie regarded her shrewdly. "Aren't you afraid that—"

"That they'd rekindle their romance?" Julia asked. "No."

In truth, she wasn't sure how she felt. Only that the longer she had to deal with Caroline Perronne, the worse she felt about herself. Maybe Caroline was the kind of woman Adam wanted in his life, after all. She certainly looked more like the woman Julia had seen on Michigan Avenue than Julia did.

It was so easy to believe that things would fall apart in the end, so easy to give in to her insecurities. Julia knew the odds. She knew how difficult it was to make a relationship work, especially when the real world intruded. Perhaps it would be best if she just accepted that fact and moved on, before she really got hurt.

She'd found herself re-evaluating her plans, wondering if Paris was the right move for her, if leaving Adam behind might be the biggest mistake of her life. Yet, she didn't want to be that woman, the kind of woman who determined her future path by the man in her life. Studying in Paris was a professional dream, something she'd been working toward since she baked her very first cake and rolled her first croissant.

"I don't trust her," Frannie said.

Julia blinked, startled out of her thoughts. With a sigh, she pushed out of the Adirondack chair and smoothed her hands over her skirt. "I don't either."

"Then why did you let him go?" Kate asked.

"I didn't let him do anything. Like Mason said, he's a big boy. He can take care of himself."

"I know what this is," Mason said. The boys had been listening to the conversation silently until now. "It's a test. You threw him into the deep end of the pool and now you want to see what he does."

Though she hadn't consciously considered that option, now that Mason had brought it up, Julia realized it was as much a test for her as it was for Adam. In her heart, she knew he'd be the perfect gentleman with

Caroline. She wasn't sure about Caroline, but that didn't really matter.

But Julia felt the ache inside when she thought about losing Adam, and leaving him to Caroline Perronne only made that ache worse. She pressed her hand to her heart. It would hurt, but only for a little while. And then, her life would go on as it had before. Romance would take a backseat to work and she'd be safe again.

"He won't do anything," Mason muttered. "He's in love with Jules."

Julia gasped. "What?"

Mason glanced back and forth between Kate and Julia. "Did I just say that out loud?"

"Say what?" Kate demanded.

"Never mind. Just rewind. Forget I said anything. That's not the kind of thing a guy is supposed to reveal."

"He told you he was in love with Jules?" Frannie asked.

"I refuse to answer on the grounds that I might piss off my best friend."

"I thought I was your best friend," Ben said.

"One of my best friends," Mason corrected.

"I'm his best friend," Kate said.

Mason leaned over and kissed his wife. "Now, let's change the subject. Do we have any more of those marshmallows, Kate? I could go for another one."

"We're all out," Kate said. "There's another bag in the kitchen. I'll go get it."

"I'll come along," Julia said.

"And I'll stay here and interrogate Mason," Frannie said.

Kate and Julia grabbed the empty cans and bottles scattered around the fire and walked up the rise to the dining hall. Kate was oddly silent and Julia was still digesting Mason's revelation.

"Do you think he actually said that?" Julia murmured.

"Why would Mason have brought it up if he hadn't? It's a good thing, isn't it?"

Julia drew a ragged breath. "I don't know. There was a time when I would have given my left and right arm to hear him say something like that. But now, it just complicates things…"

"Like what? Paris? If I had to choose between love and baking croissants, I'd choose love."

"It isn't that simple. I don't want to be the kind of woman who just tosses aside her dreams for a man. What will happen in two or three years, when he finds someone younger or prettier? And I'm left with regrets?"

Kate turned to face Julia, stepping in front of her as they reached the front door of the dining hall. "And what happens in two or three years when you come back from Paris and you realize that you let a man who truly loved you get away?"

She pulled open the screen door and Julia followed her inside. "I don't have to make a decision tonight," Julia said. "I'll just give it a little more time."

"Don't you think he deserves to know what he's up against?" she asked, as they walked to the kitchen. "You haven't been honest with him, Jules. Not about the journal or your feelings for him or Paris."

Julia tossed the bottles and cans into the recycling bin, then waited as Kate retrieved the marshmallows. "I know, I know. But I never meant for this to last. There was no need to say anything at first."

They walked back out through the dining hall. "But now it's serious. Jules, he told Mason he was in love with you."

"We don't really know exactly what he said to Mason. He could have said he loved having sex with me. Or that he loved my body. It hasn't even been a week. He can't be in love with me."

"Love at first sight," Kate said, stepping back out onto the porch.

"That only happens in the movies. Besides, I—"

A scream echoed through the still night. Kate frowned. "What was that?"

"I don't know." They ran toward the lake, meeting a drenched Caroline on the path. Water dripped from her hair as she stalked past them, her one shoe causing a distinct limp.

"What happened?" Kate asked.

"Ask Adam," she screamed again, spinning around and heaving her shoe in his direction. "Look at me. I just had my hair done today. And this dress has to be dry-cleaned. It's ruined. I'm sending him the bill. He won't be laughing then," she shouted.

Stunned, Julia and Kate watched her climb into her car and roar off down the driveway. When they reached the campfire, Adam was sitting calmly in his spot, his clothes and hair damp, a grin twitching at the corners of his mouth.

"What did you do?" Julia asked.

"She tried to kiss me," he said, the grin on his face growing. "I moved too quickly and the canoe just tipped over and we both fell in the water. I didn't realize how unstable canoes were."

A laugh bubbled up inside Julia. Adam knew exactly how to move in a canoe without capsizing it. She pictured Caroline Perronne floundering around in the water in her designer dress, her perfect blond hair hanging in strings around her face, and a giggle burst from her lips. Before long, everyone around the campfire was laughing.

"I thought you said we had to be nice to her," Mason cried.

"Hey, I was nice to her. Until she decided she was looking for a little more than just a canoe ride. Imagine my surprise. I really didn't mean to tip the canoe. You don't think I did it on purpose, do you?"

Mason pointed at him accusingly. "You're going to have to apologize for this."

"She'll get over it," Adam said. He stood up and circled the campfire to stand in front of Julia. "I think it's time that you and I went to bed." He laced his fingers through hers and drew her along toward the path to the cabins. "Good night, everyone," he called.

As they walked, he slipped his arm around her shoulders and pulled her close. "You're all wet," she said.

"Yes, but I did it for you."

"You dumped Caroline Perronne in the lake for me?"

"Well, for me, too. I didn't want to waste any more time than I had to with her. Not while I had you waiting for me. Why did you send me out on the water with her?"

"I'm sorry. I just couldn't sit there and watch her trying to get in your pants. I figured if the feeling was mutual, I'd give you a chance."

"I don't want her. You should know that by now."

Julia smiled. "I guess I do," she said.

"And don't forget it. If she comes around again, I expect you to protect me, not throw me to the wolves. Or wolf."

"I think she's more of a cougar, regardless of her age," Julia said.

He pulled her into his arms and kissed her, lingering over her lips for a long time. "You certainly do make life interesting, Jules. I'll give you that."

Julia smiled, then pushed up on her toes and kissed him again. "I think we better get you out of those wet clothes. I wouldn't want you to catch a cold."

7

Today, he smiled at me. We were working together showing the kids how to make slingshots and I made a little joke about the weapons being turned against us and he smiled. It was such a tiny thing and yet, I can't stop thinking about it. What must it be like to be the object of his attention? I've waited for so long, sometimes I wonder if it will ever happen. I know how pathetic it seems, but I still hope that someday...

THE SOUNDS OF the night filled Adam's cabin. The shutters had been thrown open to the breeze that rustled in the leaves outside.

Julia lay beside him in his bed, her naked body curled against his. She slowly traced a lazy circle on his chest with her fingertip. "Can you believe we only have two nights left? Then it's over."

Adam pulled her close then kissed the top of her head, inhaling the sweet scent of her hair. He'd want to remember all the details, he mused. Once they were back in Chicago, real life would intrude and they wouldn't be able to spend twenty-four hours a day together.

A week had seemed like forever when he'd first stumbled into her bed in the Woodchuck cabin. But the days and nights seemed to dissolve behind them until he was faced with the fact that there would be an end to this fantasy.

He grabbed her waist and pulled her on top of him, settling her knees against his hips. "If we only have two nights left, then we'd better make the best of our time." Adam pulled her down into a long, deep kiss. "Tell me that you want me."

"I do want you," Julia murmured. She shifted above him, his hard shaft pressed between her legs. "I do."

She raked her hands through his hair and returned his kiss, her tongue teasing at his. It was as if she'd sensed his worry, heard the clock ticking on their time together. It was the end of the summer again, Adam mused. It had happened this way for ten years, the waning season putting time and distance between them. But this time, it would be different. This time, their time together would continue into the fall and then the winter.

Adam cupped her face in his hands and looked into her sleepy gaze. "I'm going to miss this," he murmured. "It's been nice not worrying about real life for once."

Julia reached for him and a moment later, he was

inside her. "It has been a pleasant little fantasy," she said as she lowered herself on top of him.

They made love slowly, building the passion between them with soft kisses and gentle caresses. As he touched her, Adam memorized the feel of her body, the sound of her voice. He wanted to recall every detail. And when they finally surrendered to each other, it was as it had been from the start—perfect.

As she snuggled against his chest, Adam buried his face in Julia's hair, breathing in the scent. There were so many things he had to say to her, but he just couldn't seem to put the words into coherent sentences. He wanted to tell her how much she meant to him, yet he knew that it was too soon. He wanted to promise her that life together in Chicago would be just as exciting as it was at Camp Winnehawkee, that they could continue what they'd begun, but Adam also knew that it would probably be more difficult.

"Are you happy, Jules?"

"Umm-hmm. Very happy."

"It's a good feeling, right?"

"Yes, she said. "Of course it is."

"And I make you happy, right?"

She nodded, then pushed up on her elbow. "Where is this leading?"

"Nowhere," he said. "I just wanted to know where I stand." He paused. "Is there anything else that could make you happier than this?"

"Not that I can think of at the moment," Julia said. "But I'll let you know."

But that wasn't enough. Before they left camp, he wanted her to admit that she was falling in love with him the same way he was falling in love with her. That what they had together would survive in Chicago.

He'd been so desperate that he'd even considered proposing. If they were engaged, they'd have to spend time together. Adam had no doubt in his mind that they'd get there at some point in the future, so why waste time?

But though the plan sounded simple, Adam knew he was starting to sound like the mayor of Crazytown. Nobody proposed marriage after just five days together. What if she said no? He almost preferred not knowing how she felt to knowing that she didn't want him.

He hadn't realized until now how strong his need was. He'd do anything to be with her—anything. He'd ask her to stay, even if it meant getting rejected. The risk was well worth the reward.

But after everything he'd read in the journal, she had to love him, or at least want to continue a relationship with him. But what kind of relationship? he wondered. Sex gave Julia an excuse to think of them in only those terms—lust and release, naked bodies lost in incredible pleasure.

They had spent most of their time together in carnal pursuits. Maybe it was time for a little more romance. And perhaps she needed reminding of how she'd once felt about him. Her journal was still tucked beneath his mattress.

"I have something of yours," Adam whispered.

"You do? Have you been stealing my underwear?"

"No." He sat up, then leaned over the edge of the bed and retrieved the book. Adam held it out to her. "I believe this is yours," he said.

Julia sat up beside him, her gaze fixed on the journal. He could see the emotion in her eyes, but he wasn't sure where it came from. "I know it's about me. I read it and I recognized some of the things you wrote about."

"How long have you known?" she asked.

Adam shrugged. "Not long."

She drew a ragged breath, then took the book from him, holding it to her chest. "It's kind of pathetic, isn't it?"

"Why would you think that?"

"Did you read the whole journal? I spent ten years dreaming about you, thinking you were my Prince Charming, believing that some day we'd be together. I'd call that pathetic."

"But we are together," he said. "Isn't that what you wanted?" He reached out and touched her cheek. "It doesn't make a difference to me. In fact, I'm feeling a bit better about my prospects here."

"You don't think this is all some desperate attempt to make a teenage fantasy come true?"

"I had fantasies of my own," he said.

She gave him a reluctant smile. "You don't have to lie to me."

"It's true, Jules. I think I was probably as much in love with you as you were with me. I didn't write it all down in a journal. But you were the one girl I couldn't have, the one girl who didn't fall for my considerable charms. I used to think about you all the time, wonder what it would be like to be alone with you, to talk to you and hold your hand."

"Why didn't you do anything about it?"

"Fear of rejection," he said.

Julia ran her hand over the cover of the journal. "This doesn't make a difference, then? You don't think I'm some love-starved stalker?"

He pulled her down beside him. "I could only hope you were," he teased. "As long as it's me you're stalking, I'm cool with that."

Adam stared into her gaze, wondering what was going through her mind. He knew what was going through his. Images of her naked body, arching beneath him in pleasure, her face filled with the rapture of her release, her lips swollen from his kisses.

He didn't care how they'd arrived at this point or what had come before. They'd both had the good fortune to find each other before it was too late, before the feelings of the past had faded completely, leaving them vulnerable to others.

He was a lucky man, Adam mused. In bed, Julia was adventurous and uninhibited, driven by her desire until he had no choice but to be swept along. The way she touched him was so tantalizing that it made him hard just thinking about it. In a short time, she'd come to know his body so well that she could sense his pleasure before he fully felt it.

She ran her thumb over his bottom lip, then kissed him gently. Everything he'd ever wanted or needed in life was there in her smile, in the sound of her voice, in the feel of her body against his.

Adam had never thought much about the mechanics of falling in love, but now he wondered if it was something that occupied Julia's thoughts. He held his breath as she pressed a kiss to the center of his chest, then moved lower.

Adam closed his eyes and waited for the sweet sensation of her lips and her tongue. He'd never put much stock in the whole idea of "happily ever after." But he needed to believe it was possible. Because if there was one woman who could make him happy for the rest of his life, it had to be Julia. There was no other choice for him.

Desire was a powerful narcotic, a drug that could muddle a man's brain. But this wasn't about desire. He would he feel the same in a week or a month or lifetime from now. He knew that in his heart and yet she couldn't see it.

He wanted to tell her, to say the words out loud. But Julia was a practical girl who'd spent ten years watching him move from one pretty girl to the next. The words would hold no power unless she believed them herself.

"GET UP. JULES, wake up! Now!"

Julia squinted as she opened her eyes. Adam stood over her with a cup of coffee. Pushing aside the bedcovers, she reached out for it. "Mine or Kate's?" she asked.

"Kate's," he said. "We drank the last of yours yesterday."

She groaned, wrinkling her nose as she took a sip. It was impossible to completely wake up without her usual morning coffee. The ritual was so crucial to her mood that she'd decided, if she went to Paris, she'd have her favorite coffee shipped to her every month.

"Drink that fast," he said. "You have about a half hour."

"What time is it?" She watched as Adam rummaged around in his bag. He pulled out a wrinkled blue Oxford shirt and held it up.

"Do you think this will work? I'm going to need to iron it. I never thought to bring a business suit along." He glanced up at her. "Get up! Grace Winspear will be here in exactly an hour!"

"What?"

"Mason got the call a few minutes ago. I guess her family has a vacation home up here somewhere and she's flying in for the weekend. She wanted to see the camp on her way. So she'll be here in an hour. You're the only one who knows her personally, so I think it's important that you're there to greet her."

"An hour?" Julia jumped out of Adam's bed and began to gather her clothes scattered about the floor. "Why didn't you wake me earlier."

"He just got the call. She's flying up to Wausau and her driver will bring her here. Mason and Kate are frantic, trying to clean up everything before she arrives."

Julia gave up on trying to locate her underwear and pulled her dress on over her naked body. "I should help them."

"No, you're going to help me with the presentation. I need you for that."

"I need to bake something. She'll want coffee and she'll expect something to eat. A tarte Tatin. I have just enough time for that."

"She's not coming here to eat!" Adam said.

"I know. But you don't understand these society women. They go from meeting to meeting, nibbling along the way, sipping coffee while they get their business done. It's not like the regular business world. Believe me, I bake for them. I wonder if Kate has any apples. She loves my apple tarte."

"Jules, we can't waste time with that. I need to go over what I want you to do."

Julia hurried to the door. "You grab a quick shower and then come down to the kitchen. We'll talk while I make the tarte. Then, I'll come back up and grab a shower. We'll be ready in an hour."

"I'm not going to have time for a shower," he said.

"Take a shower," Julia said, crossing the room and dropping a kiss on his lips. "You smell like sex."

He groaned as she hurried out of the cabin, the screen door slamming behind her. Julia ran down the path toward Woodchuck, leaping over the tree roots as she went. When she walked inside Woodchuck, Kate was waiting for her, dressed in a pretty flowered dress.

"Is this all right? Maybe I should look more like a camp director. You know, polo shirt and khaki shorts."

"I think the uniform might be nice," Julia said. "Mason, too."

"Okay," Kate said. "Frannie and Ben are cleaning up the rec hall. We've got five of the sixteen cabins ready to show. The dining hall looks good, I think?"

"It all looks great, Kate. She's going to be very impressed."

Kate threw her arms around Julia and gave her a fierce hug. "Thank you. Adam told us this was your idea."

Julia smiled. "You know I'd do anything to help you guys get this camp running again. I love this place."

"So, tell me what to expect. She has tons of money, right?"

"Just be yourself. She's a really nice lady. She comes into my shop all the time and she's always been lovely to everyone. I get the sense that she maybe didn't grow up with a lot of money. By the way, do you have any apples?"

"Apples?"

"I'm going to whip up a tarte Tatin. She buys one of my apple tartes at least once a month."

Kate and Julia headed to the kitchen and before long, Adam joined them, his hair still damp from his shower, dressed in a clean polo and khakis. He sat down at the kitchen prep table, his computer open and rehearsed his presentation. Kate and Mason sat next to him, listening patiently to his advice and discussing the parts of the presentation that they'd take.

The tarte came out of the oven five minutes before Grace Winspear arrived, the black Mercedes SUV rolling up to the dining hall. They all stood on the porch to welcome her and Adam made the introductions.

"Well, this certainly takes me back," she said, looking around. "I met my late husband when he was a counselor at Camp Highland in Vilas County. My family was from the area and I used to deliver groceries to the camp kitchen. He used to walk into town on his nights off to see me." She sighed softly. "Lovely memories." She clapped her hands. "Well, let's have the tour, then."

To Julia's surprise, Grace wanted to see the entire camp from top to bottom. She chatted about her family as they walked through each building and though she was nearly eighty, she had an amazing amount of energy.

They finished the tour back at the dining hall and gathered around one of the tables. "So, why do you need money from my foundation?" she asked.

Mason cleared his throat. "We can accommodate about one-hundred and fifty campers here at Camp Winnehawkee. It's our dream to provide a camp experience for under-privileged kids," he said.

"With Mason's teaching background and my degree in social work, I think we're uniquely suited for this job," Kate continued.

"I think so, too," Grace said.

Adam continued. "The camp can be profitable with campers who pay the full tuition, which is about a thousand dollars a week per camper. The problem is, that's well beyond anything poorer families could afford. I've got a more detailed presentation for you, to show you what we had in mind," Adam said.

"There's no need," Grace said, getting to her feet. "I've seen enough. Put together a program, outline your financial needs and I'll make sure you get what you need. It's a noble cause. I'd like to see more children get a chance to experience summer camp. And I'm sure my husband would have felt the same way."

Julia stepped up and held out her hand. "Thank you, Mrs. Winspear. I owe you so much. The next time you need a cake, it's my treat."

She smiled. "I do love your cakes," she replied. "Now, I have to run. My son and his family are meeting me at our vacation home."

"Wait!" Julia said. She ran inside and grabbed the apple tarte, then quickly wrapped it in tinfoil and a paper bag. When she returned, Grace was saying her farewells.

"Tarte Tatin," Julia said. "Freshly baked. I was going to use it to convince you to say yes to our plan."

"My dear, you do know my weakness, don't you?"

Julia walked to the car with Grace. "Thank you. I can't tell you how much this means to me and my friends."

"It's going to be a lovely place," she said. "You take care, dear. I'll see you back in the city."

Adam stood at her side as they watched the car disappear down the driveway. When it was finally out of sight, Mason let out a whoop and picked up Kate, spinning her around in a wild embrace.

Julia glanced up at Adam and smiled. "I guess we did it," she said.

He leaned close and brushed a kiss across her lips. "You are amazing," he murmured.

"No! You're amazing," she teased.

"We're both amazing. And we make a really good team." He cupped her face in his hands and kissed her again, lingering over her mouth for a long time. "I do love you, Jules."

Julia didn't have time to respond. Kate joined them and gave her a hug, then kissed Adam on the cheek. "Let's go get Ben and Frannie. We need to celebrate. I think we should go out dancing tonight."

"I think we should take the rest of the day off,"

Mason suggested. "We'll do some waterskiing and drink some champagne and—"

"We don't have champagne," Kate interrupted.

"We'll go buy champagne," Adam said. He grabbed Julia's hand. "Come on, Jules. My wallet is up in my cabin."

"Right," Mason called as they hurried toward the path. "The old wallet in the cabin trick. Don't fall for that one, Jules, it's the oldest play in the book."

When they reached the privacy of his cabin, Adam drew her into his embrace again. "Thank you," he murmured, his lips brushing against hers as he spoke. "Thank you, thank you," he added between kisses.

"I gave you a name," she said. "I didn't do that much."

"I'm thanking you for me, now," he said.

"You?"

"For the first time in my professional life, I feel like I've actually done something that I consider worthwhile. And I couldn't have done it without you. We did good today, and I haven't been able to say that since I left camp."

"We did do good," Julia agreed. "It's the perfect ending to a perfect week."

"It's not over yet," Adam said. "We still have tonight and tomorrow night."

But it was almost over, Julia mused. And before long, all the worries of the real world would intrude and distract. Though she wanted to believe what they shared would survive sixteen-hour work days and weekends spent at the bakery and out-of-town business trips, Julia refused to be too optimistic.

If he truly was in love with her, then things weren't going to get easier. They were about to become much more complicated.

But the more she tried to talk herself out of being with Adam, the more Julia realized that she'd gotten herself so tangled up in him there'd be no way out. She'd done it again, only this time she'd known better. She was an adult and should have been able to control her feelings. But from the moment they'd first made love, she'd been lost.

All her talk about keeping things simple between them had been part of the wall she'd tried to build. But faced with the reality of their situation, that wall had crumbled to rubble in front of her. Her body belonged to him, along with her heart and her soul, and Julia knew that was all her fault. She'd fallen in love with Adam.

It wasn't so hard to imagine them together. She'd always run her life with such single-minded determination, but now, she couldn't even make a simple decision about her happiness. She had to trust her feelings and, ultimately, trust him. He wasn't a boy anymore and Adam knew what he wanted. He wanted her.

With exquisite ease, he worked his way up until he pressed a kiss beneath her ear. And then, as if he'd already tired of the game, he grabbed her waist and pulled her toward the bed. He kissed her mouth, his tongue tangling with hers, the sweet taste of the whipped cream passing between them.

He sat down, Julia straddling his lap. For a long time, they kissed, exploring each other's mouths until they'd perfected the act itself.

If she could spend the rest of her life kissing Adam, Julia knew it would never become routine. Every touch sparked her passion and elevated her need until she was frantic for a more intimate connection. But what if they didn't have the rest of her life? What if today and tomorrow were all they had?

She slowly undressed him and then fell back onto the bed, his body sinking down on top of hers, his hips settling between her legs. But as he brought her closer and closer to her release, Julia realized that what they were doing was wrong.

They were both trying to act as if it was just passion and lust driving them forward, that what they were doing was sex and nothing more. But she knew it wasn't true. The emotional connection was still there, the force that had brought them together in the first place. No matter how much they both tried to ignore it, it wasn't going to go away.

And when it was over and she lay sated in his arms, Julia knew that they hadn't had sex. They'd made love.

ADAM FLOATED LAZILY on an inner tube, his eyes closed against the afternoon sun, the gentle undulation of the water relaxing his body to the point of sleep. Julia and Kate sat on the end of the pier, dangling their feet into the water while Mason, Ben and Frannie were somewhere on the lake waterskiing.

He felt perfectly content. Everything in his life was working, moving in the right direction, and he felt as if he were along only for the ride.

After tonight, they had just one more day and night at the camp. By Friday morning, he and Julia would be headed back to Chicago. Though he'd tried to picture himself in the city with her, the images seemed unfocussed. He wasn't sure who she was in the city. He knew virtually nothing about her job, her friends, her apartment. He didn't know the restaurants she frequented or her favorite shops. It would be like getting to know her all over again.

Waiting until dinner on Sunday night to see her was hard. But he'd need to learn to live with the time apart. A day or two wasn't going to be as difficult as a month or two. But then, if they lived together, they'd see each other much more often.

He thought about the options. His condo was in Lincoln Park which would be the logical place for them to reside, but her flat was within walking distance to the bakery, which made her life a lot easier. He could always sell and move into her neighborhood.

Adam groaned softly. It was easy to get ahead of himself. Right now, they had a date for dinner and he was already making plans to relocate. "Slow down," he said to himself. "One day at a time."

The sound of an engine grew in volume and Adam

turned his head and watched as Mason brought the boat closer to the pier. He flipped the inner tube and swam to the ladder, climbing out in time to grab the lines from Frannie and knot them around the cleats on the pier.

He held out his hand and helped Frannie from the boat. "Anyone else going out?" he called. "Jules, you want to try?"

"I'm a miserable failure at waterskiing," she said with a shrug. "I'd only humiliate myself."

"But I love watching you humiliate yourself," he teased. "It's so much fun."

"I'm glad I amuse you." She stuck out her tongue at him, then turned back to her conversation with Kate.

"Come on," Mason said to Adam. "Come out with me and Ben. One spin around the lake."

Adam undid the lines, then pushed the boat away from the pier. Mason slowly backed it into deeper water, then swung the wheel around and hit the throttle. The boat skimmed across the water as Adam stood in the cockpit, the wind blowing his hair back, the cool spray on his face.

When they reached the far side of the lake, Mason slowed the boat and let it drift. He sat down, stretching his legs out in front of him. "I'm going to miss having you guys around," he said. "You'll have to come back for the grand opening next month. You'll get to see the camp in operation."

"I can come," Adam said. "What about you, Ben?"

"I'm sure I can get off."

"And you'll bring the girls, right?" Mason asked. "Kate will want them here."

Adam nodded. "Yeah, I'll bring Jules."

"Is she even going to be around?" Ben asked. "Frannie told me that she's going to France to study pastry-making."

Adam frowned. "Yeah, but I don't think that's for sure."

"Frannie seemed to think it was. She's talking about going for a year or two. How are you going to handle that?"

Adam sat down next to Ben, bracing his hands on his knees. "A year or two? She mentioned Paris, but I thought it was more like a vacation." He turned to Mason. "Has she said anything to Kate?"

"Well, yeah. But I just assumed her plans would change now that you two are together."

"We're not officially together," Adam muttered.

"That's good," Ben said. "It's kind of hard to be together when one of you is in Chicago and the other is in France. And what about this dude she's going with? Frannie says—"

"What dude?" Adam asked. He turned to Mason, who shrugged.

"I haven't heard about any dude," Mason said.

"Old boyfriend," Ben said. "French guy. Baker. Jean-Claude."

Adam cursed beneath his breath. Well, there it was. It figured once he thought things were going well, they'd all come crashing down on top of him. Julia had mentioned Paris, but she'd left out a lot of the details. It was no wonder. How the hell did she think he'd react?

Right, Adam thought to himself. Here he was caught up in planning for the future while she knew she wouldn't even be in the country. She'd warned him from the beginning. This was just a week out of time and he'd lost sight of that.

"Should we go back in?" Mason asked.

Adam shook his head. "Naw. I'm all right. I just got a little ahead of myself, that's all. She's a very…captivating woman."

"Hey, don't take my word for any of this," Ben said. "I may have it wrong. I mean, I'm not really used to having a woman talking to me twenty-four-seven. I admit, there are times when I tune Frannie out."

"I was wondering about you two," Adam said. "You guys are sort of in the same situation. What happens when you go home?"

Ben forced a smile. "Frannie has made it clear that she's only using me for sex. But I'm kinda thinking that she likes me. I'm not going to try to figure her out. I'm just happy to have a woman in my bed, for however long it lasts."

"So you haven't fallen in love with her?"

Ben laughed. "Hell, no. It hasn't even been a week. It's going to take a lot longer than that for me to learn to tolerate her bullshit. She is just about the bossiest woman I've ever met."

Maybe he *had* jumped too soon, Adam mused. Ben had it right. Keep his distance and let time sort it all out. But then, Ben's relationship with Frannie was all about the sex. Adam knew that he and Jules had something deeper.

"Are you sure you don't want to go back in?" Mason asked.

Adam shook his head. "I'm cool. I could do some skiing."

In truth, he needed a while to chill. If he went back now, he'd just drag Jules off to some place private and demand answers, answers that he wasn't sure he wanted to hear. For now, he'd re-evaluate his options.

8

*I haven't written in this journal for almost eight years.
Though my last entry seems as if it was written by a
stranger, I still recognize so much of that girl still alive
inside of me. Have I really changed at all? I still have
the same fears and insecurities, but I'm strong enough
to know that they can't hold me back. I'm falling in
love, not with the boy of my dreams, but with the man
he's become.*

JULIA RAN HER hand across the page of the journal. It
felt good to write in it again. Almost as if things had
come full circle. When she'd left the journal behind on
her very last day at camp, she thought she was closing
a chapter in her life. But now, she realized that the story
hadn't been finished.

She'd have to make a decision about Paris before
long. She'd already talked to her shop manager about
taking over the bakery while she was gone. She'd also

made plans to sublet her apartment. And Jean-Paul had found her a small studio apartment to rent near her bakery in Paris. If she backed out at the last minute, it would cause a few problems, but it wouldn't be a disaster.

But she didn't want to back out. Julia wanted to go to Paris *and* she wanted to be with Adam. She wanted to be wildly in love for the first time in her life and she wanted to lose herself in a study of French pastry. She wanted it all.

She flopped back in her bed and stared up at the ceiling. So much had happened in a week. She thought she'd turned her life upside down when she decided to go to Paris. But now, it was spinning in a totally new direction.

The ring of her cell phone interrupted her thoughts and Julia searched for the phone. She found it on the floor next to the bed and immediately recognized the number from the bakery.

"Hi," she said. "What's up?"

Her manager, Jessie, was on the other end. "We've got a problem," she said, the tone of her voice sober.

Julia sat up, her mind on alert. "What is it?"

"The oven is out. It's been heating unevenly and we were dealing with that but now it doesn't heat at all."

"Did you call the service tech?"

"We did, but the part is on back order."

"You'll have to bake in the small oven," Julia said.

"We have been, but that's put us way behind on decorating. We're not going to get the cakes done for this weekend. Everyone is working, but we're running way behind. We can't possibly have them all ready in time."

Julia stood up and began to gather her things from around the cabin. "I'll be home by eight. Don't rush. I don't want the cakes to look sloppy. And call in Marco. Pay him whatever he wants."

"All right," Jessie said. "I'll see you soon."

Julia hung up the phone and tossed it on the bed, then grabbed her bag from the floor. She ought to have let the problem solve itself, she mused. If she went to Paris, she wouldn't be available to rush home to help. But the need to please her customers overwhelmed her practical thoughts. She didn't want to be the cause of a bride's unhappiness on her wedding day.

As she tucked the journal into the bag, Julia heard the screen door open behind her. When she glanced over her shoulder, she found Adam standing there, his hair wet, his feet bare and his expression stormy.

"Who is Jean-Claude?" he asked. "And why are you going to Paris with him?"

Julia gasped. She hadn't expected that question. "Jean-*Paul* is an old friend and teacher and I'm not going to Paris with him, I'm going to Paris at the same time as him."

"Don't mince words with me, Jules. He's your ex. And when were you going to mention that you'd be gone for a year?"

"I haven't decided that yet," Julia replied. "Who told you about Jean-Paul?"

"Why am I the last to find out about this?"

She reached for her bag and began to stuff her clothes inside. "I didn't think it was important. I haven't made any firm decisions yet."

"You leave in a few months," he countered. He paused, as if he'd just realized what she was doing. "Why are you packing?"

"I have to go back. There's a problem at the bakery and if they don't have my help, they won't finish the wedding cakes for this weekend. I don't have any choice."

"We need to sort this out, Jules."

"There's nothing to sort out. I haven't decided what I'm going to do yet and I have to leave."

"But you're still considering the trip. So why did you let me go on and on about us and our future? Was this some kind of grand plan to pay me back for all those years at camp?"

She gasped. "What? You think this is all some kind of revenge?"

"I don't know, Jules. I don't know what to think. When were you going to tell me about Paris?"

"I did tell you!" she cried.

"And you left me with the impression that you'd be gone a week or two. And you didn't tell me about the guy, this Jean-Claude."

"Jean-Paul. His name is Jean-Paul."

"Good to know," Adam muttered. He cursed softly. "Let me ask you this. If this hadn't happened between us, would you be going to Paris for a year?"

Julia closed her eyes. He wanted honesty, but she knew what that would mean. "Yes," she said. "I've been ready to go for about six or seven months. It's all been planned."

"And this was important to you?"

Julia nodded. "It's been a dream of mine. For a long time."

She saw the conflict in his expression and she wanted to reach out and reassure him of her feelings. But his arms were crossed over his chest and he looked unapproachable. "You need to go," he said. "Back to Chicago. And you need to go to Paris."

With that, Adam turned around and walked out of the cabin. Julia ran to the door. But she fought the urge to call out to him. Maybe it was best to put some distance between them. She needed time to figure out what all this meant. They'd been on a runaway train and it was time to hit the brakes. It was time to come back to reality.

"Welcome to the real world," she murmured.

At first, Julia had convinced herself that a week with Adam would be enough to last her a lifetime. But having a week with him was almost worse than never having had the time together at all.

She turned away from the door and walked back to the bed, then sat down on the edge. This felt like love, or as close to love as she'd ever been. But how much of that was real and how much imagined? How could she tell the difference? Paris had been her dream for so long, a plan for her future, and now she was willing to throw it all away for a possibility.

Common sense told her that she'd regret staying, that someday, after Adam was out of her life, she'd realize she'd made the biggest mistake of her life—and over a man.

"Jules?"

Julia closed her eyes at the sound of Kate's voice. "Come on in."

"What's going on?"

"I have to go back to Chicago," Julia explained as Frannie and Kate walked inside. "Trouble at the bakery."

"Is everything all right with you and Adam?" Frannie asked. "He just took off alone with the boat."

"No. I guess one of the boys must have mentioned my trip to Paris and I really hadn't told him about that yet. It's my fault. I should have been honest with him."

"But you'll work things out, won't you?" Kate asked.

"I don't know. I need some time. This has all happened so fast. I feel like I've been living in a dream."

Kate reached out and gave her a hug. "I wish you could stay."

"Me, too," Julia said as she hugged Frannie.

"Will you come back for our grand opening?" Kate asked.

"I'll try," Julia said. She grabbed her bag, then drew a deep breath. "I have to go."

Frannie and Kate gave her another hug. "We'll walk you out."

As they strode down the path to the dining hall, Julia breathed in the last memories of the camp. The feelings rushing through her were so familiar, a sense of loss and emptiness. As a girl, the last day of camp was the worst day of her year and it felt that way now.

Mason and Ben were waiting at her car and they both gave her a hug. "Tell Adam I said good-bye and I'll talk to him in Chicago."

"I'll do that," Mason said.

"I'm sorry," Ben said. "I should have kept my mouth shut."

Julia forced a smile. "It's all good. I should have told him myself. You just made things a little easier for me."

She gave them all a little wave as she drove out, steering the Subaru down the winding road. Her thoughts returned to the drive north from Chicago. She'd been so excited to revisit the past at Camp Winnehawkee. But her past had become her present. Was she willing to make it her future, too?

ADAM STARED AT his computer monitor, re-reading the letter of resignation he'd written. He'd been back in Chicago for twenty-four hours, but it was long enough for him to realize that he needed to make a change.

The long ride home was a perfect time to examine the choices he'd made in his life. He could trace his unhappiness back to one point—taking a job with his father's firm. He was tired of making money for money's sake.

A week with Mason and Kate was all it took to see that true happiness would only come from doing something he had a passion for. Finding investors for shopping malls and condo complexes didn't fit the bill.

At the same time, he'd decided what made him completely happy in life. Julia. Such a simple answer to what he'd been searching for. And though their relationship was fractured for the moment, he knew he could make her see that they belonged together.

He pushed a key, then waited for the letter to print. A signature on the bottom made it official. Adam folded it and put it in an envelope with the company logo printed in the corner.

He'd already packed the few personal items he'd brought to the office and they sat in a box on the corner of his desk. It was Saturday morning and the office was as busy as any weekday. Adam smiled to himself. Until he found a new job, he had Saturdays off. Along with the rest of the week.

He tucked the box under his arm, then walked down the hall and stopped at the desk of his father's secretary. She glanced up at him and smiled, noticing the box. "Doing some house-cleaning?" she asked.

"You could say that," Adam replied. He held out the envelope. "Give that to my father when he gets out of his meeting, would you, please?"

"No problem," she said, setting it on her desk. "Did you have a nice vacation?"

"I did," Adam said. "Probably the best vacation I've ever had."

"Where did you go?"

"Just a quiet little spot," he said. "It wasn't really the setting but the people I was with."

"Well, time to get back to the grind."

"For you maybe," Adam said. He walked down the hall, nodding to people as he passed their offices. Some of his coworkers called out to him as he passed but Adam kept walking. The closer he got to the door, the more he felt a sense of freedom lightening his spirit.

It was a perfect summer day and he had it all to himself. But he had only one place that he wanted to be. He found his car in the parking ramp and dropped the box in the trunk, then headed out of the Loop toward Wicker Park.

Adam turned up the radio, listening to the Sox broadcast and wondering if he ought to take in the second half of a double header. Or he could grab his bike and head down to the lakefront for a long ride.

It took him fifteen minutes to reach Damen Avenue from his office. He scanned the string of storefronts in the trendy neighborhood, searching for the correct address and when he found it, he pulled into the next parking spot available.

He got out of the car and slowly walked down the street, stopping at a coffee shop situated directly across from Julia's bakery. La Dolce Vita was lettered on a sign across the facade of the shop. The sweet life. He smiled. A perfect description of their time at Camp Winnehawkee.

Adam walked inside the coffee shop and ordered an Americano, then recognized the taste the moment he took a sip. This was Julia's coffee, the kind she made for him that first night in the cabin. He walked back outside and sat down at one of the café tables set up on the sidewalk, his gaze fixed on the bakery.

They'd made a date for tomorrow night and he had every intention of keeping it. He'd made a reservation at a trendy restaurant for seven and planned to show up at her flat at 6:30 with flowers and the hope that she'd at least let him in the door.

Everything had happened so fast on Thursday, between his finding out about her Paris trip and her having to leave, that they hadn't gotten anything settled between them. But he'd decided it wasn't absolutely necessary to figure out everything right away.

Now that he was unemployed, he had no responsibilities, no ties to Chicago. If she wanted to go to Paris, he could hop on a plane with her. He had plenty of money in his investments and savings to live very comfortably for at least two or three years, longer if he scrimped a bit. And if he sold his house, he'd have even more.

It was time he had an adventure. He'd played the dutiful son for eight years, long enough for any man to put off starting his own life.

He hadn't realized until now how strong his feelings were. He'd do anything to be with Julia—anything. And it had nothing at all to do with their physical attraction. He missed talking to her and listening to her voice, watching her move across a room or smile at him.

Adam had to believe that Julia just hadn't figured it all out yet. She was still fighting her feelings and when she finally reconciled herself to the fact that she might be in love with him, too, then everything would be clear.

Great sex had given Julia an excuse to think of them in only those terms—lust and release, naked bodies lost in incredible pleasure. The kind of desire they shared would distract anyone—including him. When they saw each other again, he had to try a different approach. And for that to work, he'd have to keep his clothes on and his hands off her body.

The front door of the bakery opened and he picked up a newspaper from the table next to his and opened it, peering over the top as he saw two women run across the street. They were both dressed in pink chef coats and wore pink bandanas twisted through their upswept hair.

Julia looked so beautiful, yet like a woman he barely knew. He didn't recognize the clothes or the serious look on her face as she talked to her coworker. She was so absorbed in her conversation that she didn't even notice him as they walked in the front door of the coffee shop.

Adam watched her through the window as they ordered a pair of iced drinks, still caught up in their conversation. Though he wanted to go inside, to act as if their meeting was completely by chance, he knew that wouldn't fly.

Instead, he watched her surreptitiously, taking in every detail of her face and body. His fingers twitched as he remembered what it felt like to touch her.

When she walked out again, he nearly called her name. The urge to walk over to her and pull her into his arms was almost too much to resist. But he'd decided to control his physical needs the next time he saw her. They needed time to get to know each other outside the bedroom.

Okay, so now he knew where she worked. And she lived just a few blocks away. Adam picked up his coffee and walked back to his car. He'd cruise past and get familiar with the neighborhood, then check out some of the restaurants in the area. If he was going to spend more time in this neck of the woods, it would be a good idea to see what it offered.

As he walked down the street, Adam stopped at the window of a jewelry shop. He stared down at a pretty bracelet and wondered if he ought to go inside and buy it.

He'd been on a lot of first dates in his life, but this one was important. In a way, it was the beginning of their relationship out in the real world. He wanted it to be a fantasy for her, the kind of night she might have dreamed about when she was younger and madly in love with him.

But was a gift appropriate or was it too much? What about the flowers? Could the bouquet be too big? Adam cursed beneath his breath. Hell, he wasn't even sure they still had a date. He'd been afraid to call her and confirm for fear that she'd break their plans.

He felt edgy, maybe even nervous, at the prospect of ringing her doorbell. Would she be expecting him? Would she smile when she saw him? Hell, he wasn't even sure what kind of food she liked to eat. Reaching into his pocket, he pulled out his cell phone and dialed Kate's phone.

Kate was Julia's best friend. If she couldn't fill him in on the necessary details, then no one could.

JULIA STOOD BENEATH the shower and tipped her face up into the warm water. Every bone in her body ached. She couldn't remember the last time she'd worked these long hours. She'd left camp on Thursday evening, worked all night long and through the next day, had three hours of sleep on Friday night before heading back to the shop at 3:00 a.m. Saturday morning.

Saturday night was spent prepping for Sunday and on Sunday morning, she'd worked the counter. After all that, she had curled up on the sofa in her office and fell asleep until late afternoon.

There was one benefit to being so busy. She hadn't had much time to think about Adam—or Paris. But now, exhausted and alone, thoughts of him flooded her mind. Like a delicious home movie, images drifted through her head, the memories sending a flood of need racing through her.

She ran her hands over her body, her fingertips skimming wet skin. His hands, his touch, his kiss, it all came back, the need causing an ache deep inside of her.

They'd made plans for dinner that evening, but Julia hadn't heard from him since she'd left camp. They hadn't parted on good terms and no doubt, he was still stinging from the revelations about Paris. She didn't blame him. Keeping him in the dark had been a bad decision on her part.

Though she'd thought about calling him, Julia had decided to put a little space between them, at least for a while. It was so hard to think about moving to Paris when all she wanted to do was spend the next year or two in his bed. He was a distraction that made a decision impossible.

Once she had a clear mind, she'd be better prepared to chart her future. She ran her hands through her hair, then leaned back against the tile wall. She'd always been so careful, so controlled. Emotion had never had an important place in any decision she'd ever made.

Julia shut the water off and stepped out of the shower, then wrapped herself in a thick terry robe. She grabbed a towel and squeezed the water out of her hair, then wandered out into the kitchen. The Sunday paper sat unread on the island.

She pulled a sport drink out of the fridge, glancing up at the clock. Before she'd gone into the bathroom, she'd ordered Thai noodles from a local restaurant and the meal was due to arrive before long. As she took a long drink, Julia thought about where she and Adam might have dined.

In truth, Julia was glad the date had fallen through. She wasn't sure what she wanted to say to him, and until she was, it was better to avoid any contact. She didn't know when she'd be ready or when he'd decide he was prepared to forgive her.

The doorbell rang and she pulled the robe tightly around her as she walked to the door, her bare feet quiet on the cool wood floor. Grabbing her purse from the floor beside the closet, she dug through it for her wallet as she opened the door. But her favorite delivery man wasn't standing on the other side.

Her breath caught in her throat as her gaze met his. For a long moment, she forgot everything that had happened between them. The joy of seeing him again nearly overwhelmed her and she had to stop herself from throwing her arms around his neck and kissing him.

"We said seven, right?" Adam asked. He pulled a huge bouquet of flowers from behind his back and handed them to her. "I hope you like flowers." He shrugged. "That's one of the things we never talked about. Whether you liked flowers."

"Did we still have a date?" Julia asked. "I hadn't heard from you so I thought we—"

"Of course we did," Adam said. "But you're not ready yet. I can wait."

She stepped aside to let Adam in, but as he passed her, he paused. Their gazes met and for a long moment, they stood perfectly still, neither one of them able to move.

The flowers fell to the floor and Adam pulled her into his arms and kissed her. It wasn't like any other kiss they'd shared before. This one was filled with desperate longing and frantic need. They'd only been apart for a few days, but Julia felt as if it had been years.

She hadn't remembered how wonderful it felt to touch him or taste him, how his mere presence made her knees go weak. They stumbled until she stood, her back against the wall. His fingers wove through hers and he pinned her hands on either side of her head as he deepened his kiss.

The tie from her robe had come undone and the terrycloth parted, revealing her naked body beneath. This only seemed to make him more determined to possess her, and Julia couldn't think of a single reason to resist.

She struggled with the buttons of his shirt and when she couldn't get them all undone fast enough, he yanked it open, the buttons scattering on the floor. Smoothing her hands over his chest, she drew back and kissed him there.

She thought about taking him to the bedroom, but she was afraid to speak or even move, knowing that the mood that had fallen over both of them might vanish in an instant.

He slipped his hands around her waist and drew her

up against his. Julia felt completely vulnerable, her naked body open to his touch while he was still clothed. And yet, the thought of making love to him like this sent a thrill through her.

She reached for the button on his jeans and undid it with clumsy fingers. She dispatched the zipper just as quickly and a moment later, wrapped her fingers around him.

He groaned and Julia slowly began to stroke. But Adam wasn't content to just enjoy her caress. He found the spot between her legs, now damp with desire. She closed her eyes, a shiver skittering through her body.

After just a week together, they'd grown to know each other so well and within minutes, they were both hovering on the edge of their release. When he picked her up and wrapped her legs around his waist, Julia expected him to carry her to the bedroom.

But instead, he positioned her above him until he could slowly push inside of her. Julia held her breath as he allowed her to sink even lower, the sensation of him filling her driving her even closer to the edge.

When he could go no farther, he drew a deep breath and let it out slowly, as if to control his urge to move. But Julia didn't want to wait. They could take things slow the next time. Right now, she needed to feel him moving inside her, needed to experience his orgasm along with hers.

He slid his hands over her hips, cupping her back-side as they began to move. Desire washed over her in waves. Though she wasn't trying to exert any kind of control, she was in charge, able to control their pace and the depth of his penetration.

His lips continued to return to hers again and again, as if he needed to reassure himself that she was still all right with what they were doing. How much more could she give him, Julia wondered. Her body was his, her soul, her heart. But yet, there was something left to surrender—her dreams.

Was Adam her dream, was he what she'd been waiting a lifetime for? The last week had seemed as close to a dream as she'd ever experienced in life. But six days was such a short time. And Adam had always had a way of making her lose sight of the person she was.

Julia knew that love could be fickle and fleeting, and even if they stayed together now, they might not be together later. He was obviously willing to try, willing to give her whatever she needed to make it work.

He reached up and cupped her face in his hands, drawing her down into a long, deep kiss, tasting her sweet mouth. "I love you," he murmured against her lips.

The words came so naturally now, without even a second thought, that Julia knew they were real and not just a spontaneous outburst.

"I love you, too," she said.

He drew back and looked into her eyes and when he was satisfied that she was telling the truth, he began to move again, this time, with more purpose.

Julia held his face in her hands, their gazes locked. Every moment of pleasure could be read in his expression and she watched as he came closer and closer to losing control.

Though she wasn't concentrating on her own response, she felt the need inside her intensify, pushing her toward the inevitable. But Adam wasn't ready yet and he held tight as he carried her to the dining room table.

He set her on the edge and then gently pushed her back until her body was open to his gaze and his touch. And when his fingers found the spot between her legs, Julia moaned, the sound coming as a surprise to her.

Her breathing grew shallow and quick and she whispered his name softly, her fingers gripping the edge of the table. He was close to his own release, but Adam had turned his attention to her. Their coupling grew in intensity and became wild and uncontrolled. They spoke to each other in ragged fragments, the words the only thing keeping them tethered to reality.

And then she was there, arching against him and crying out his name. An instant later, Adam dissolved into powerful shudders. She let herself go, tumbling over the edge in a free fall of pleasure as he drove into her again and again, burying himself to the hilt, until they were both completely spent.

She thought they'd experienced the heights of pleasure already, but Julia realized that tonight, they'd broken through a wall and reached an entirely different level. They hadn't been driven solely by physical desire. Their bodies had touched in the most intimate fashion possible, but this time, so had their souls.

He leaned over her and kissed her softly. Julia wrapped her arms around his neck as his lips trailed over her shoulder. The doorbell rang and the sound startled Adam, but she held tight to him.

"If you tell me that's another boyfriend, I'm not going to be happy," he murmured.

"Thai Express," she said. "Pad Thai noodles with shrimp."

He pushed up, bracing his arms on either side of her body. "I could eat," he said, sending her a boyish grin.

"You could? You could eat right now? You're hungry?"

"Well, yeah. Kind of. And Thai noodles sound pretty good."

Julia giggled.

"No, no," he said, as he slipped out of her.

"You need to zip up and get the door before he goes away."

"And you better cover yourself up. I don't want to give the noodle man an eyeful."

Laughing, Julia sat up and pulled her bathrobe around her naked body. When Adam was dressed again, he opened the door and paid for the take-out. He turned back to her and Julia watched him, her legs dangling from the edge of the table, her hands braced behind her.

"You know, those noodles are really good cold."

"What are you suggesting?"

"I haven't shown you my bedroom yet."

"Oh, you haven't." He tossed the bag on the table, then picked her up and set her on her feet. "Show me the way."

With another laugh, Julia raced ahead of him, but he caught up with her after just a few steps and carried her the rest of the way.

Though she had tried to resist, there was no denying it anymore. Adam belonged in her life. They were meant to be together. But could she put aside one dream for another? Or was there a way she could have everything she ever wanted?

9

Life used to be so simple when I was a kid. Everything was black and white, decisions easy to make. But now, faced with the biggest decision of my life, I'm afraid to take a step in either direction. I never used to understand why some women insisted on trying to have it all. But then, I've never been in love. Can I have it all, or will I be forced to choose? And if I have to choose, will the choice be for me or for us?

ADAM SNUGGLED BENEATH the covers of Julia's bed, pulling her into the curve of his body and slipping his leg between hers. They'd spent the night together and were now enjoying a lazy Monday morning in bed.

It felt strange not to have to worry about going to work. Strange, but enjoyable, Adam mused. He'd discussed his decision with his father Saturday night and they'd managed to agree to disagree on his choices. But

Adam wasn't going back, no matter what his father offered him.

"Why is it so cold in your apartment?"

"I have the air conditioner set really low," she said. "I spend my day around hot ovens and in the summer it can get pretty brutal in the bakery. I just like it to be cold when I sleep."

"You don't have air conditioning in the bakery?"

She shook her head. "In the shop we do. And in the cake decorating room, but nowhere else."

"Tell me more about this bakery," he murmured, pressing a kiss to her shoulder.

"What do you want to know?"

"What do you make there?"

"Lots of things. Cinnamon buns, morning buns and—"

"What are morning buns?"

"They're like a cinnamon roll only instead of frosting, they're covered with cinnamon and sugar. They're really good. Very crispy on the outside"

"Do you have some here?"

"No," Julia said, laughing. "I try to keep baked goods out of my house. I'd get really chubby if I ate everything I baked."

"I'd still love you if you were chubby," he teased.

"You would not."

"I would," he said, a serious expression on his face. "Really, Jules. It wouldn't make a difference. I want to grow old with you. And we're not always going to look as wonderful as we do now. I'll love you, no matter what."

She ran her hands through his hair. "Will you love me if I decide to go to Paris?" Julia asked.

He hadn't realized until this moment that it didn't make a difference if they had to spend some time apart. People in love survived long distances all the time. And he was willing to do whatever it took to make her happy.

"I will. In fact, I'll love you even more if you decide to go to Paris."

"Really?" she asked.

"If Paris is where you need to be, then that's where you have to go, Jules. I'm a big boy. I can survive on my own until you get back."

He wanted to tell her about his altered job status, about the fact that he could come to Paris with her, but Adam decided that this time, he'd be the one keeping a secret. She needed to make this decision without any convincing from him. Once she'd decided to go, then he'd invite himself along.

"I meant what I said," he whispered. "I do love you."

"I know. And I love you."

A long silence grew between them and Adam knew there was more to say. Julia snuggled closer and kissed his chest. "Do you worry that it happened too fast?"

Adam rolled over on his stomach, determined to look into her face as they spoke. Her eyes were wide, watching him warily. "I don't know that we had any control over that. Some people fall in love quickly, others take time. I do know I've never said those words before to a woman and I'm pretty certain that you're the last woman I'll say them to."

"We've only known each other for a week."

"We've known each other for years, Jules," he countered.

"But that doesn't count."

Adam laughed sharply. "Why the hell not? It should count for a lot. You know me, Julia, and you know that I'll do everything in my power to make this work."

Julia sat up, pulling the bedcovers up around her naked body. "How? Tell me how it will work. Make me understand."

"I can't," he said. "I don't really know exactly how things will go. If I did, I suppose that would take all the excitement out of actually living our lives together. But, I do know that I don't want to be with anyone else but you. So we'll find a way." Adam watched her, waiting for a reply, some sign that she was thinking about what this meant.

Julia nodded. "All right. I guess that's good, then. We'll just let things unfold and see where they go."

"That's the plan," Adam said. "Now, what's the plan for breakfast? I'd love some of those morning rolls."

"We probably have some day old ones at the bakery. If you get dressed, we can walk over and I'll feed you a proper breakfast of coffee and pastries. And since the shop isn't open yet, we'll have the place to ourselves."

Adam smiled and rolled out of bed. "Let me get dressed."

Julia watched him from the bed as he collected his clothes and pulled them on. He rolled the shirt sleeves of his cotton shirt and slipped on his loafers without socks, but he was ready in less than a minute.

Julia crawled out of bed and pulled a clean bra and panties from the top drawer of her dresser. Adam crossed the room. "Is this it?" he said, pulling the drawer open again to peer inside. "Oh, look at this. My fantasy come true. A woman who has fancy underwear."

"It's my only vice," Julia said. "Since I'm forced to wear a uniform all day long, I like wearing nice under- wear beneath."

"You didn't bring any of this stuff up to the cabin," he said. He pulled out a red bra, trimmed in black lace. "I definitely would have remembered this," he said, ex- amining it closely.

"Get out of my drawers," she said.

He grabbed her around the waist as she pulled a cotton dress over her head. When her face appeared, he dropped a kiss on her lips. "I was in your drawers earlier and you didn't seem to mind."

"Very funny," she said.

"I just want to get to know you a little better," he said.

"And what can you tell about me from my underwear drawer?"

"That hiding beneath that very cool, collected exterior, there's a wild and wanton woman aching to be free."

She slipped into her sandals and grabbed a light sweater. "You have no idea," Julia teased.

The weather was cool and breezy when they got outside, the sky a dull gray as if a summer shower were approaching. Adam grabbed her hand as they walked.

"When do you think you're going to leave for France?" he asked. "Is the date set yet?"

"Around the first of September."

"Then you'll be around for the grand opening at Winnehawkee."

"Kate sent me a note, but I'm not sure I'll be able to go. It depends upon what's going on at the shop. We've brought in a new pastry chef and I need to make sure he's up to speed before I leave."

"So we have about seven weeks left. We can have a lot of fun in seven weeks."

They chatted about their week at camp as they walked the three blocks to Julia's shop. They entered through the front door, Julia locking it behind them. The interior was dark and cool. "I can't turn on the lights or we'll have people knocking on the door to get in," she said.

"Don't let anyone in," Adam said. "Not until I've eaten all the cinnamon rolls I want."

He walked along the glass cases that lined one side of the shop. Though most of the trays were empty, there were still a few treats left. Julia stepped behind the counter and put his choices in a flat pink box with the shop's logo printed across the top. When he'd made all his choices, they walked back to the kitchen where she made a French press of coffee.

This was what Monday mornings would be like, he mused as he slowly devoured a morning bun. At least for the next seven weeks. They'd spend Sunday nights in bed and Monday mornings sharing breakfast at the bakery.

She glanced over at him and smiled and he licked the sugar off his bottom lip, a reminder of their recent activities. A pretty blush stained her cheeks and Adam felt a bit sinful trying to tempt her in her place of work. But at this point, he was willing to take any opportunity offered.

As Julia rose to fetch another cup of coffee, Adam noticed an odd expression on her face. Sadness, tinged with regret.

"Are you all right?"

Julia nodded. "I'm just a little tired."

"You know, I think these pastries would taste much better eaten in bed. We can go back to your place and spend the day pretending it's Sunday. You had a *Tribune* on the kitchen counter. We'll read that and be lazy all day long."

"Don't you have to go to work?" she asked.

Adam shook his head. "Nope. Not today I don't."

A weak smile curled the corners of her mouth and she took another deep breath. "You're too good to me,

Adam Sutherland," she said. "Who would have thought you'd grow up to be such a nice man?"

THE INVITATION FOR the Camp Winnehawkee grand opening arrived via email with a long note from Kate begging both her and Adam to attend. At first, Julia had sent her regrets, faced with a week from hell at work and no way to make it up north by Saturday afternoon.

Adam had stopped at the shop before he left last night, kissing her good-bye and promising to wish the first batch of campers good luck. But as she finished up one of the Saturday wedding cakes, Julia realized that she didn't want to be in Chicago, not when all her friends were gathered at the camp.

She'd paid her employees overtime to stay and finish the cakes, then took off just after 4:00 a.m. on Saturday morning. Though she had to stop three times to catch a few minutes of sleep, Julia turned into the driveway of Winnehawkee an hour later than her expected arrival.

She hadn't bothered to tell anyone she was coming. But she knew they'd all be pleased. Still, she hadn't come just for Kate and Mason, or for Frannie and Ben. She come because she'd finally made her decision about Paris.

She'd decided to try it for six months. Six months wasn't that long and the time would fly by quickly. If, after six months, she couldn't stand to be away from Adam any longer, she'd come home. If not, then she'd invite him to visit. And if she made it through the first six months, she'd try another six months. Just giving herself the option to change her plans was enough to make leaving Adam possible.

Until the moment she'd decided, Julia had tried to put their relationship in its proper perspective. It had been just a momentary fling, an affair that had a beginning and an end. But then they'd fallen in love and everything had changed. And yet, the more time they spent together, the more she realized that Adam wasn't standing in the way of her dreams. He wanted her to go.

Falling in love hadn't been an ending but a whole new beginning. Julia had found herself believing in a future with him. Not just a weekend here or there, or a vacation together when they both had time. She was starting to think this might be something permanent, something that might last a lifetime.

She'd reached for the phone countless times, ready to call him and beg him to come with her. But then, she realized that Paris was her dream, not his. She had to believe him when he said they'd make it work.

As if by instinct, she started to get that trembling feeling of anticipation, the same feeling she'd had as she drove to the north woods the first time. The weather was warm, the breeze was blowing through the windows of the car and her friends were waiting for her.

But tonight, she and Adam wouldn't sleep in a cabin. He'd reserved a room at one of the resorts, trying to tempt her into attending. Little did he know he'd be sharing his bed with her tonight.

Her cell phone rang, startling her out of her thoughts. She picked up her phone. "Aren't you supposed to be busy?" she said.

"You should be here," Kate replied. "Especially since it was you who found Mrs. Winspear. She's here, you know."

Julia smiled at Kate's familiar voice. "I know. She stopped by the shop on Friday to pick up the cake. Have you seen it?"

"It's so beautiful," Kate said. "Thank you. You do too much for us."

"Is Adam there?"

"Yes. Frannie has been parked on the dock with a novel. Ben and Adam are out waterskiing with a couple of guys from town."

"Well, go call Frannie and have her come up to the dining hall," Julia said.

"Why?"

"Just call her. It's important." Julia slowed the car on the drive up to the camp. She heard Kate shouting in the background and a minute later, Frannie got on the phone.

"You are the biggest party-pooper I know," Frannie said. "How could you stay home? We all want you here."

"All right," Julia said. "Fine. I'll come."

Frannie gasped. "You will?"

"Yes," Julia said. "If I leave right now, I should be there in...wait a second...oh, my God. I'm here already. Look, there's my car. Driving up the path. It's really me."

Frannie screamed into the cell phone as she turned to see Julia's car pull up to the dining hall. They came running up to her as she got out and gave her a group hug. Julia laughed. "Am I still a party-pooper?"

"No," Kate said. "You're my best friend forever."

"Mine, too," Frannie said.

They walked into the dining hall and Julia checked on the cake, relieved to see that Mrs. Winspear's drivers had managed to get it from her car to the plane and back to the car again without any major mishap.

"Did Adam know you were coming?" Kate asked.

"Nope. I really thought I'd have to work. But we finished everything very early this morning."

"How are things between you two?" Frannie asked.

"We're in love," Julia said, pressing her hand to her heart. Frannie and Kate stared at her, stunned by her admission. "Don't look so surprised."

"But what is this going to do to your trip?"

"I'm still going," Julia said. "I leave on September third."

"But that's good," Frannie said. "I mean, now that Adam has quit his job, he can come and see you more often."

"What?"

"Well, he'll have a lot more—"

Julia frowned. "What did you say about his job?"

"That he quit his job?" Frannie cursed. "Don't you

guys ever talk about stuff? I mean, it's hard to be your friends. I feel like we know more about what's going on with you two than you do."

"Adam quit his job the day after he got back from camp in July," Kate said. "He told us last night. We assumed you knew."

"No. I mean, I just assumed he was going to work. What has he been doing?"

"Maybe you should talk to him," Kate suggested. "Every time we get caught in the middle of something, you end up mad at each other."

"I—I'm not mad. I'm...stunned," Julia said. "Why would he quit his job?"

"I think he was sick of it," Frannie said.

"Do you think he quit so he could come to Paris with me?"

"Ask him!" Kate and Frannie said in tandem.

"All right. Where is he?"

"Waterskiing. Go down to the end of the pier and maybe you can wave them in when they drive past," Kate said. "Then sort out your stuff and get back to us."

Julia smiled. "I'll do that."

ADAM BOBBED IN the water, the tips of the skis breaking the surface. He adjusted his grip on the tow rope then waved his hand at Ben. His friend shoved the throttle forward and the boat sped off. A moment later, the rope jerked and pulled Adam to his feet.

He skimmed across the glassy surface, weaving back and forth across the wake, absorbing the bumps with his knees and sending a huge plume of water out behind him as he carved into his turns.

Though he was having a good time, he couldn't help but wish Julia had been with him. Right about now, she'd be making her Saturday deliveries, loading the wedding cakes into the bakery's two panel trucks and dropping them off at various locations around town.

Then, she'd prep for the Sunday morning opening before going home for an early supper and bed by 7:00 p.m. He already knew her schedule well, well enough to know that she'd be waiting for his phone call around seven.

As Ben turned the boat back toward Winnehawkee, Adam glanced toward the shore. The camp was filled with new campers and guests who had come to participate in the grand opening festivities. Mason and Kate were rushing around, getting some of the seventy-five campers settled while their church leaders were going over the activity schedule with their counselors.

Renting the camp to the church group had been a perfect chance for a dry run before they opened the camp to regular campers. They'd decided to begin small, with just 75 kids in the one and only two-week session which would begin the first of August. But next summer, they'd have a full schedule, thanks to Grace Winspear.

Ben looked back at him and twirled his finger, wondering if Adam wanted to complete another trip around the lake. He nodded, but as he skied past the Winnehawkee pier, he recognized a familiar figure standing on the end. He wiped the water from his eyes and looked again. It was Julia, or someone who looked remarkably like her.

Adam let go of the towrope and glided into the pier, dropping below the surface just a few feet away from the ladder. He raked his hand through his hair as he stared up at her.

"What are you doing here? I thought you had to work."

"I didn't want to miss a weekend with my friends."

"Your friends?" he asked

"And you," she said. "I don't like sleeping alone anymore."

Adam grinned, then kicked off the skis. He handed them to her before he climbed up the ladder and stood in front of her. "You wanna get wet?"

"You gonna make me wet?" she countered.

He pulled her into his arms and kissed her. She drew back, then looked around to see some of the kids watching them from the beach. "I think that will do for now," she whispered.

He took in the sight of her beautiful body, schooling the urge to touch her at will. He felt a pulsing warmth rush through his bloodstream and pool in his lap. Though they'd enjoyed each other in bed Thursday evening, it didn't seem to make a difference. Thankfully, he was wearing baggy board shorts that hid his reaction.

"I'm glad you're here," he said.

"Me, too." A tiny smile quirked the corners of her lips. "Because if I wasn't here, you wouldn't have a chance to explain."

"Explain?"

"Yes, explain. Why you quit your job and didn't tell me."

"Oh, right. Well, I was going to tell you. But then, I decided not to because it really didn't make a difference. And I didn't want you to think I was some kind of lazy bum, because I'm not. I just decided it was time to make a few changes in my life." He shrugged. "Like you going to Paris."

"What have you been doing with your free time?" she asked.

"I've been working out a plan for the campers' program with Mrs. Winspear's people. I've been riding my bike and reading a lot. Managing my investments. And spending every possible moment with you."

"You've been busy," she said.

He grabbed her hand and pulled her along the pier. "We need to get out of here."

"I just got here," Julia said.

"Then we need to go find somewhere where we can be alone. I want to kiss you again."

"I don't need you to kiss me, Adam. I need to know why you didn't tell me you'd quit your job."

"I'll explain. I promise." He dragged her along to the boathouse, then tested the door. It was unlocked.

Adam opened it and pulled her into the dark interior. He leaned forward and brushed his mouth against hers. He'd intended the kiss to be simple and quick. But the moment their mouths touched, a current of desire passed between them. It was as palpable as heat lightning on a humid summer night, startling and intense.

Adam grabbed her waist and pulled her against him, kissing her again, this time more deeply. She immediately opened to his assault, as if she were desperate to taste him, too.

His hands skimmed over her body, feeling the familiar curves. She was dressed in a thin, cotton shirt and shorts that hugged her hips and her backside, but it wasn't difficult to imagine her body beneath, all soft skin and naked flesh.

"It's strange," he said. "I feel like I used to on that first day of camp, when I'd see you after nine months apart. I'd spend hours thinking of a clever opening line that was both funny and charming. And then I'd chicken out."

"You should have tried kissing me," Julia murmured.

"I can see that now." Adam walked across the room and slipped his hands around her waist. "How have you been? And don't tell me about work."

"I'm currently feeling very…confused," Julia said. "I guess that's the best word for it."

"After being around you and seeing how much you loved what you did for a living, and how much Mason and Kate loved the camp, I wanted to feel that same thing, too. I was working for my father out of obligation, not out of any sense of passion for the profession."

"Don't you have bills to pay?"

"Let's just say, I've invested very wisely. I have plenty of money. And when I run out, I'll get another job."

With a trembling hand, she reached out and smoothed her palm over his chest. Her fingers traced a path between his collarbone and his belly. Adam closed his eyes and enjoyed the feel of her touch.

"I came up here to tell you something," she said. "I've made a decision about Paris."

He opened his eyes. "You have?"

Julia nodded. "I'm going for six months. I'm going to leave on the third of September."

"Good," Adam said. "You've made the right decision."

She paused, studying his face in the dim light from the boathouse door. "You know, if you're not working and don't have anything better to do, you—" She paused and took a deep breath.

"What could I do, Jules? Tell me."

"You could always…"

"Come to Paris with you?"

Julia nodded. Her brow furrowed with worry and he knew she wasn't at all sure of the answer he'd give. "Would you like that?"

"Yes, I would like that very much. I think we could have a wonderful adventure there."

"I think we could, too." He pulled her into his arms. "Yes, Jules, I'll go to Paris with you."

Kissing her had always been a wonderful prelude to other activities, but this time, Adam made sure that the kiss was enough to convey his feelings. He lingered over her mouth, softly drawing his tongue over her lower lip. When he finished, he kissed the tip of her nose. "I love you, Jules."

"I love you," she replied.

"You can speak French, can't you?" he asked.

"Enough to get by in a bakery and on the street," she said. She sighed. "We're going to have to find another place to live. I only have a very small studio apartment."

"Well, I'll have to get on that."

A flutter sounded above their heads. Adam looked up to see a bat in the rafters. Julia screamed and ran out of the boathouse, flailing her arms around her head. Adam followed her and slammed the door behind him.

"Isn't this where we started?" Adam asked.

Julia brushed her hands through her hair. "Except I hit you on the head with a tennis racquet."

He took her hand. "Come on, Jules. If we're going to spend the rest of our lives together, we might as well get started now."

"Where are we going?"

"I don't know. But wherever it is, it's going to be a lot of fun."

Adam glanced over at the beautiful woman who stood at his side and grinned. A man could do just about anything with a woman like Julia in his life. And he couldn't imagine anyone he'd rather spend the next sixty or seventy years loving.

Epilogue

SPRINGTIME IN PARIS was more beautiful than Julia ever imagined it to be. The cold, damp winter had finally given way to warm, sunny days. The cherry trees were in bloom around Notre Dame cathedral and the tables outside the cafés were crowded again. All over the city, people were tossing aside their coats and scarves and strolling the boulevards in their best spring fashions.

Julia drizzled the last of the glaze on top of the _tarte aux pommes_ and then slipped it into the glass display case. Wiping her hands on her apron, she glanced around the shop. Everything was in place for the late afternoon rush, which meant she was done with work for the day. Stretching her arms above her head, she smiled to herself. _"C'est fini,"_ she called to her boss.

"Formidable," he said, poking his head out of the workroom at the back. "See you tomorrow, Jules."

"À demain, Henri." She took off her apron and tossed it over her shoulder, then picked up her bag from behind the counter. As she headed out the front door, she grabbed a baguette from the basket near the cash register. Tomorrow was her birthday. No doubt, they'd have a cake and a celebration for her at the bakery. And Adam had promised that a gift would be arriving for her before the big day.

Julia had been in Paris since September, living in a fifth-floor walk-up in the sixth *arrondissement* and working in a bakery just a block from her apartment. She'd settled into life and work with little trouble and had decided to learn the French language—first, as it applied to baking and after that, as it applied to life. She finally realized her progress just a few days ago on the *métro* when she was able to eavesdrop on a conversation between two women and understand what they were gossiping about.

Professionally, her life had never been better. She had learned so many new things about breads and pastries and cakes and fillings. She'd even signed up for a few evening classes at a Paris pastry school. A whole new world had opened up to her and every week, she spent a few hours on video chat with her staff back home, relaying new techniques and ideas.

Unfortunately, her romantic life had hit a few bumps along the way. Adam had planned to move to Paris a month after she did, but when his father fell ill, he'd been forced to stay in Chicago and help run the family business. They'd existed on long internet chat sessions and daily phone calls, gifts sent back and forth and the occasional love letter.

She'd spent a grand total of twenty-two days with him in the past eight months, ten in Paris, four in London, five in Barcelona and a quick weekend in New York. The wonderful adventure that they had planned together had been delayed time and again, replaced with a series of passionate rendezvous in hotel rooms.

She hadn't seen him in more than a month and he'd canceled last night's internet date because of a problem with his computer. It was getting more and more difficult to be away from him and Julia had already decided that a year in Paris would have to be enough. By the end of the summer, she'd head back to Chicago, back to her business and back to the man she loved.

By the time she reached her apartment, she had already calculated the time difference between Paris and Chicago. It was about time for Adam to get up and go to work. She might be able to catch him before he left. Right now, she needed to see his face and listen to his voice.

She walked through the carriage door that led into the inner courtyard of her building, then unlocked the door to the stairway up to her apartment. After daily trips up and down five flights, her butt muscles had begun to look better than they ever had before, a good thing since she'd added a baguette to her daily diet.

When she reached the fifth-floor landing, she unlocked her front door and stepped inside the silent flat. As she walked inside, she tripped over something sitting on the floor. Cursing softly, she looked down to see a familiar leather duffel sitting in the hallway. "Adam," she murmured. Her pulse quickened and she hurried inside, ready to throw herself into his arms.

Julia found him sound asleep on her bed, still completely dressed and wearing his shoes. She knelt down beside him and stared at his handsome face. She couldn't think of anything she wanted more for her birthday than a visit from Adam. Leaning over, she pressed a kiss to his cheek, inhaling the scent of his hair as she did.

Straightening, Julia kicked off her shoes and slipped out of her white jacket, then carefully crawled into bed next to him. He stirred as she snuggled against his body and then opened his eyes.

"Hi," she said.

He smiled sleepily. "Hi."

"You're here."

"Happy birthday," Adam said. He leaned toward her and touched his lips to hers, smoothing his hand over her cheek.

Julia sighed softly and closed her eyes. "I've missed you so much." Adam wrapped his arms around her and pulled her close. There was nothing that felt better than this, she mused. And though it had been almost two months since she'd last touched him, now that he was here, it seemed like just yesterday.

"How long can you stay?" Julia asked.

"Forever," he murmured.

She frowned. He'd never given that answer before. "How long is forever?"

"As long as the French government says it is," Adam teased. "Probably three months for a tourist visa. If you want me to stay longer, you're probably going to have to marry me."

Julia gasped. "Marry you?"

Adam groaned. "Did I just ask you to marry me?"

"Yes," she replied. "No. Not exactly."

"Forget I said that. I shouldn't have said that."

She frowned. "All right."

"Sorry." He kissed her again, then held up a small velvet-covered box he'd pulled from his pants' pocket. "This is how I was supposed to do it." Adam braced himself on his elbow, then opened the box and pulled out a beautiful diamond ring. Julia watched, stunned, as he reached for her hand and slipped the ring over the tip of her finger. "I should probably be down on one knee," he said.

"No," Julia replied. "I like this."

"All right," he said, nodding. "Now that I have the ring, and I'm finally going to be living here in Paris, I think it's about time to make things official. Julia McKee, fellow camper and love of my life, will you marry me?"

"You're really going to stay this time?"

"Yes," he said. "My father is back at work, so I'm done."

"Would they really kick you out if we don't get married?"

"I have no idea," Adam replied. "Are you going to give me an answer, or would you like to sleep on it?"

She held her hand out, staring at the sparkling diamond set in platinum. "It looks perfect," she said. "Like it's supposed to be there."

"It is. The minute I saw it, I knew it was the right ring for you. Now, are you going to give me an answer? Or are you going to torment me for a little while longer?"

Julia stared into Adam eyes. "I would love to marry you, Adam Sutherland."

He grabbed her around the waist and pulled her on top of him, capturing her lips in a long, delicious kiss. It was the kind of kiss she'd expect from a man completely and utterly in love. When he finally drew back, she was breathless, her heart pounding in her chest. It had been the perfect proposal—a bit unconventional, but still perfect in every way.

"You know, I'm going to have to write all about this in my journal."

"Make sure you leave out that first part and start with the ring," Adam suggested.

Julia shook her head. "I'm going to write it exactly how it happened. Because that's the way I'm going to remember it."

She curled up in the curve of his arm, her face pressed against his chest. They'd have time to celebrate later. Right now, she wanted to fall asleep in his arms. And when she woke up, Adam would still be there… this time, for the rest of her life.

* * * * *